SPECIAL MESSAGE TO READERS

THE ULVERSCROFT FOUNDATION
(registered UK charity number 264873)
was established in 1972 to provide funds for research, diagnosis and treatment of eye diseases. Examples of major projects funded by the Ulverscroft Foundation are:

- The Children's Eye Unit at Moorfields Eye Hospital, London
- The Ulverscroft Children's Eye Unit at Great Ormond Street Hospital for Sick Children
- Funding research into eye diseases and treatment at the Department of Ophthalmology, University of Leicester
- The Ulverscroft Vision Research Group, Institute of Child Health
- Twin operating theatres at the Western Ophthalmic Hospital, London
- The Chair of Ophthalmology at the Royal Australian College of Ophthalmologists

You can help further the work of the Foundation by making a donation or leaving a legacy. Every contribution is gratefully received. If you would like to help support the Foundation or require further information, please contact:

THE ULVERSCROFT FOUNDATION
The Green, Bradgate Road, Anstey
Leicester LE7 7FU, England
Tel: (0116) 236 4325
website: www.ulverscroft-foundation.org.uk

THE WISHING TREE

Grieving photojournalist Jake Allen is determined to remain Hawthorn Ridge's recluse — until spirited Emma Brinkley moves next door with plans to reopen the beloved Wishing Tree Children's Nursery. Despite her own sad secret, Emma's warmth chips away at Jake's defences, even as challenges test her resolve. When a storm and a health scare threaten everything Emma has worked for, Jake steps in as her unexpected hero. Together, they discover that love — and community — can heal even the deepest wounds.

CHRISTINA HOLLIS

THE WISHING TREE

Complete and Unabridged

LINFORD ROMANCE

LINFORD
Leicester

First published in Great Britain in 2023 by
D.C. Thomson & Co. Ltd.
Dundee

First Linford Edition
published 2025
by arrangement with
the author and
D.C. Thomson & Co. Ltd.
Dundee

A catalogue record for this book is available from the British Library.

ISBN 978–1–4448–5560–9

Published by
Ulverscroft Limited
Anstey, Leicestershire

Printed and bound by CPI Group (UK) Ltd.,
Croydon, CR0 4YY
This book is printed on acid-free paper

MIX
Paper | Supporting responsible forestry
FSC® C013604

New Beginning

Emma's stomach began to grumble. She checked her watch and gasped.

'No wonder I'm hungry — I haven't had anything to eat since breakfast!'

Living on fresh air, mugs of tea and the excitement of moving house was not a good idea. Making herself something to eat would take time, though, and Emma didn't feel up to puzzling out the workings of her new home's cooker.

What she needed right now was a treat. Something from the village fish-and-chip shop could be her housewarming present to herself.

She grabbed her handbag.

Closing the front door, she ran down the steps, turned and looked up at the old, red-sandstone building.

This year had started with heartbreak for Emma. It was the end of summer now and a new chapter was opening in her life.

'If Leonard hadn't called off our

wedding I would never have discovered that Great-aunt Elizabeth went through the same thing back in the Seventies,' she told herself.

Elizabeth South was a very private person, but had opened up to Emma in a letter after hearing that her great-niece's wedding had been called off.

It had marked a turning point for both women. They bonded over their disappointments and also discovered they shared a love of children.

Elizabeth owned a pre-school nursery in the village of Hawthorn Ridge. The Wishing Tree Nursery was based in what had once been Hawthorn Ridge's Methodist chapel.

On reaching retirement age she had cut back her activities and the nursery was now a once-weekly drop-in for mums and toddlers.

'I couldn't find anyone to take on the business,' she confided in Emma. 'Well, not anyone I thought would put children before profits. All the applicants were too much like my ex-fiancé for my liking.'

'I know what you mean,' Emma had replied sadly.

When Elizabeth had asked if she might be interested in taking on the business, common sense had warned Emma to curb her enthusiasm.

She had let her heart rule her head over getting engaged, after all. Discovering how deep the pool of disappointment could be had been a terrible shock.

On the other hand, the bank branch where Emma worked was marked for closure so she would need another job soon.

'All you'd need to do is supply refreshments and healthy snacks for the mums and little ones each Thursday morning, Emma.

'You'd be offering the village a service by keeping their social group going.'

That would be good for Emma, too.

Taking a deep breath, she had agreed to try running her aunt's business.

And now here she was, in Hawthorn Ridge at the beginning of her new life.

No Secrets

There was a queue in the village take-away. Emma took that to be a good sign. The food must be worth waiting for!

The delay was torture. She had far too long to study the mouth-watering menu with its images of juicy chicken and thick, home-made burgers.

By the time the child in front of her staggered off, carrying a family-sized order, Emma was almost faint with hunger.

She opened her mouth, ready to give her order, but the girl behind the counter smiled and shook her head.

'Sorry. There will be a bit of a wait for the next batch of chips.'

Emma looked longingly at the crispy bits the girl was fishing out of the fryer and dropping into a takeaway tray.

'Back in Bristol we call those scrumps,' she remarked. 'You're not going to waste them, are you?'

The girl grinned and wrapped the

discarded fragments into a little parcel that she lodged on top of the heated display cabinet to keep warm, along with other orders for collection.

'No way,' she replied.

An older woman emerged from the back of the shop to see how business was doing.

'You must be the girl who's moved into Miss South's old place.' She smiled.

'Yes! How did you know?' Emma asked.

'You can't keep secrets in Hawthorn Ridge. Let me take your order. What can I get you, my dear?'

'I'd like a large haddock and fries, please, with —'

Before she could finish speaking, the door burst open. She swung round to see what was happening.

A tall, good-looking man with dark hair strode up to the counter, wallet in hand.

'Evening, Mrs Chatterton. Evening, Alice.' He waggled a bank card at them.

'Excuse me, I was here first,' Emma protested.

The man silenced her with a hard stare.

Laughing, the young assistant smiled at the handsome man.

'Dinner for one and a half again tonight, Mr Allen?'

'Got it in one, Alice.'

The girl picked up one of the large packets from the top of the display cabinet together with the smaller parcel of scrumps.

She popped both into a small carrier bag and handed it to him.

'There you go, Mr Allen.'

He tapped his bank card against the payment machine and swept out.

That left Emma hungry, annoyed and curious, too.

'Was that Mr J.P. Allen of Plum Tree Cottage, by any chance?' she asked.

'The same,' Mrs Chatterton confirmed. 'You're his new neighbour. And I'd say you were in enough trouble with him already, without accusing him of queue-jumping!'

Emma went hot then cold all over.

'What kind of trouble?'

'He was the only person who objected when the planning committee discussed your application to fill the old Methodist chapel with pre-schoolers again.'

Emma gasped.

She had been busy since accepting her aunt's offer.

After researching the area, she'd contacted the local primary school. The headmistress had confirmed there was a desperate need for childcare in the village.

A new company had opened on the outskirts of Hawthorn Ridge. There were jobs for all who wanted them, but many found the lack of nursery places a problem.

The Wishing Tree Nursery seemed exactly what this village needed.

She had spent weeks researching how to get the business started again and reviving all the permits and permissions she needed.

'You are right about there being no secrets in this village, then.'

That could work to her advantage. If news about the nursery was already doing the rounds it might bring in enquiries from parents.

'It would have been more of a surprise if Mr Allen hadn't kicked up a fuss, to be honest.' Alice handed over Emma's order.

'He's a local. We're all very protective of our village,' Mrs Chatterton added. 'Mr Allen moved down from Hawthorn Ridge Farm to get some peace and quiet.'

She and Alice exchanged knowing looks.

Emma gave a rueful sigh.

'And then he discovers that a nursery might be opening up next door. Not only that, but it would be run by an incomer to the village, too!'

'That's right.' Alice shut the till with a snap.

If the staff in the chip shop knew who Emma was, then Mr J.P. Allen probably knew it, too.

He couldn't have missed seeing the small van and two huge removal men who had carried Emma's things into the old chapel that morning.

She stepped out of the shop and into the late August evening.

She had to walk right past the front gate of Plum Tree Cottage to reach her new home.

'I should have made a point of calling in and introducing myself straight away,' she told herself. 'I don't want to start off on the wrong foot.'

After passing his cottage, she paused and looked back.

It should have been the easiest thing in the world to open the garden gate, walk straight up the path and introduce herself, but Emma couldn't quite bring herself to do it.

As she hesitated, a light went on in one of the downstairs rooms.

J.P. Allen was probably as keen to tuck into his supper as she was, she decided with relief, hugging her own warm paper parcel of fish and chips.

She would call round first thing tomorrow. Yes, that would be best. She would be feeling braver by then . . . she hoped.

J.P. Allen

Next morning, Emma awoke to warm sunshine streaming through her bedroom window. For a split second she wondered where she was.

Then she remembered this was the first day of her new life in Hawthorn Ridge.

She shivered with excitement — and worry. The first thing she had to do this morning was to go and introduce herself to Mr J.P. Allen.

Why hadn't she done it last night? Those takeaway suppers would have given them both the perfect excuse to keep the meeting short.

Tense with nerves, she didn't feel much like breakfast. Every spoonful of cornflakes felt like a bucket of rubble.

As she did the washing-up she stared out at the old stone wall separating her new home from Plum Tree Cottage.

If she delayed too long he might have gone out. Although it would be a relief to find he wasn't home, that would only prolong her agony.

Leaving the breakfast things to drain, she dried her hands and set off before she could lose her nerve.

At the gate of Plum Tree Cottage she put her hand on the catch, then stopped to take in the scene.

Mr J.P. Allen's house was as pretty as its name. Its front garden billowed with arching wands of shrub roses that stood knee-deep in a jumble of dahlias and phlox.

Gravel that must once have been a driveway was quilted with heartsease, alchemilla, and wild strawberries. A plum tree heavy with ripening fruit leaned over the patchwork of plants.

A Red Admiral butterfly fluttered down to inspect the darkening purple skin of a sun-kissed plum. Emma watched it, fascinated.

She ought to get a tree like this, she thought. It would attract butterflies and she could make fruit juice for the children.

Opening the garden gate of the cottage was difficult. Its hinges had dropped and the rusty catch was a poor fit.

Once inside, Emma had to wrestle the gate shut again over the rutted gravel path.

The squeaking, scraping sounds started a dog barking somewhere behind the house. Before Emma had time to react a dark shape streaked around the side of the building.

As the dog bounded towards her, the front door of Plum Tree Cottage flew open.

'Tiger!' a stern voice warned.

The brindle crossbreed skidded to a halt. As sleek and shiny as a well-filled sausage, it thrashed its tail in greeting.

Emma could only focus on its impressive array of teeth.

'Is it safe?' she asked.

Clicking his tongue irritably, J.P. Allen strode down the path and clipped a lead on to his dog's collar.

'Of course he's safe.'

'Sorry. I didn't know whether to

believe the noisy end of your dog or the wagging one.'

He pointed toward the gate.

'Didn't you see the sign?'

Emma turned, confused.

'I didn't see anything.'

He advanced, the dog pattering along beside him. Emma had to move aside.

Her neighbour prised his garden gate open with a flourish, then frowned.

'Ah, it appears to have fallen off.'

Bending down, he retrieved a small rectangle of plywood from the pavement. The words 'Beware Of The Dog' were painted on it in bold, black letters.

Her neighbour was as tall and impressive as she remembered from their first meeting at the chip shop. He seemed an impressive dog-handler, as Tiger was now sitting at his feet and looking up at him adoringly.

Emma still wasn't confident.

'So he doesn't bite?'

The dog cocked its head and looked at her. Its expression was more grin than growl.

'Of course not! Who in their right mind keeps a dangerous dog?'

His expression made Emma rally. He might not want to build bridges, but that wasn't going to stop her trying to sort things out between them.

She took a deep breath.

'I'm Emma Brinkley. We met in the chip shop?'

She had hoped he would respond but was disappointed. He stayed silent, his mouth a tight line of disapproval.

Taking another deep breath, she pressed on.

'I know we got off on the wrong foot, Mr Allen, and that you have objections to what I want to do. If the nursery causes you any problems I'd like you to come and see me straightaway. I'll try to sort something out.'

Gabbling the words all in one go left her gasping for breath.

'You'll try?' His blue eyes were as cold as sky reflected in ice as he gazed down on her.

'I know you objected to my planning

application.' She tried to smile. 'I want to make sure we stay on friendly terms.'

Neither she nor Mr Allen were impressed with her efforts, clearly.

For the first time Emma began to feel self-doubt about her hopes and dreams

'I'm reopening Wishing Tree Nursery.'

She cocked her thumb feebly in the direction of her new home and business.

'I know. I saw you moving in.'

'OK. Well, I want to show you that I'm not a monster.'

She frowned, wondering where those words had come from. Her recent experience of men — at least, one man in particular — had left her convinced that Mr Allen was much more likely to prove the villain than she.

'I never thought you were, Miss Brinkley,' he said finally. 'I objected to your application because I didn't want my peace and quiet wrecked by an incomer.

'Someone who is likely to move on after five minutes when they don't manage to make a fortune overnight!'

Future Problems

Emma tilted her chin. She could almost feel herself growing taller with indignation.

'Do I look like I might do that kind of thing, Mr Allen? Like you, I'm all for a quiet life.'

'Yet you are about to fill your house with children,' he retorted.

'That's an exaggeration. The number of children will depend on how many qualified staff I can employ, but it won't be more than twenty.

'The walls are thick and double-glazing on the windows means most of the noise will be contained. The children will only be outside during their breaks, or storytime during nice weather.'

'As well as when they arrive and leave each morning and evening.'

This man was impossible!

'That's only twice a day. Won't you be out at work during those times, Mr Allen?'

'I work from home. The last thing I want is a stream of cars arriving and leaving right outside my house.'

Reasonable. Luckily that had been the first problem Emma had considered.

'I'm going to suggest parents carpool where they can. There's lots of parking on the waste ground at the edge of the village, too, a couple of hundred yards away.

'I'll be running a reward scheme. A child will get a gold star every time they walk to the nursery rather than come by car.' Her smile was wide and genuine.

She looked down at the dog at his feet.

'You might not like children, Mr Allen, but it seems you like animals. When I heard about your objection I scaled back my own plans of keeping chickens.

'I had been hoping to give the children a taste of caring for pets and seeing how eggs are produced.'

He smiled back at her, which was such a surprise that Emma gasped.

'Good idea. Nobody could object to that — not even me.' He shrugged. 'After all, you're in the country now.'

'Really?' Emma was wary. 'I assumed you'd complain if you were woken up by crowing every morning.'

'If all you want is eggs, rather than chicks, you won't need a cockerel. A few hens wouldn't bother me.'

'You're sure you don't mind?'

'It's your property — you can do what you like. As you've proved over your plans for expansion,' he added.

'That's only to give me more space, not the children. At the moment I'll be living over the shop, so to speak.

'Once I've got the business up and running I'll move into the renovated outbuilding.'

'In that case you'd do well to hold off keeping chickens until you've finished all the repairs. The chickens would thank you for it. And you'd thank me for the advice.'

She had the impression a smile was never far from his lips despite his serious expression. It was waiting to appear like the sun from behind a cloud.

'You know about chickens and that kind of thing, then?'

'Enough to know that you'll have no end of trouble with not-so-little visitors if you don't have a good clear-out first.

'Miss South was a lovely woman, but the place was alive.'

Her look of puzzlement made him smile.

'She used to keep poultry in those old sheds herself. Wherever there are hens there are lodgers.'

Emma frowned, still confused.

'Samuel Whiskers,' he elaborated.

'As in Samuel Whiskers, the rat in Beatrix Potter's story?' she asked slowly.

She felt he was the last person in the world to know about children's books.

'You mean there are rats in those sheds?'

'Not any more. They are clever creatures so they'll have moved on.

'If you keep chickens or feed wild birds, the food spilled will always attract four-footed burglars — unless you are careful.'

Emma shuddered.

'Don't let me put you off,' he added. 'As you say, it's good for children to care for animals. As long as you take precautions and make everything rodent-proof it'll be fine.'

She tried a smile.

'Then could I ask you for some advice?'

His icy gaze reappeared for a moment, then thawed by half a degree.

'Such as which comes first, the chicken or the egg? Well, that depends on how keen you are on raising your own chicken dinners.'

Emma drew in a sharp breath.

'Not at all! I mean, I love roast chicken but I couldn't eat one of my own birds.'

'Yes, you strike me as the sort of person who would say that,' he said with an air of superiority.

She felt heat in her cheeks.

'I have to think of the children, too. Some of them are bound to be vegetarian.'

He snorted.

'The only vegetarians I know of around

here are either teenagers or incomers.'

'I'm an incomer and I'm not a vegetarian!'

'You amaze me,' he drawled.

'My concern is that I'll be looking after other people's children. I have to be aware of all the likely pitfalls.

'Nuts will be banned — that's a given. But I'll also be offering gluten-free versions of any food I give to the children. It's what people will expect.'

'You can spend too much time thinking about other people,' he told her with a thoughtful look in his eyes. 'You aren't a bit like I imagined you'd be, Miss Brinkley. I assumed you'd be a ditzy blonde.'

It was Emma's turn to purse her lips.

'When you run a business —'

'— like you do,' he interjected with a gleam in his eye.

She fixed him with a look and continued.

'You have to be sensitive to other people's needs.'

He cleared his throat softly.

'You haven't been running your own business for long, have you?'

Emma toyed with the idea of admitting it, but his high-handed manner was annoying.

'That has nothing to do with it.'

'Listen, one of the first things anyone learns when you start working for yourself is that you're going to need all the goodwill you can muster.

'If you keep in mind that I'm the hermit of Hawthorn Ridge it's possible we'll get along . . .'

'Just fine?' she prompted brightly.

He refused to be brightened. His mouth returned to its grim line.

'I like routine, Miss Brinkley.'

'So do babies and toddlers, Mr Allen.'

Emma returned his scrutiny with interest.

'I'm going to give you a copy of our timetable before we open so you can know what to expect and when.'

She should stop talking, she decided. This man looked as though he expected the worst every minute of every day.

'I don't like noise,' he warned.

This was bad. Racket was the specialist subject of every little child!

She couldn't argue against that, but she tried anyway.

'I guarantee that all you'll hear from the Wishing Tree Nursery will be happy sounds.'

He looked down his nose at her.

'You sure about that?'

Transatlantic Call

Jake Allen retreated into his house and closed the front door with a thump.

Releasing Tiger from his leash, he walked back into his sitting-room.

Tiger had hopped into his basket beside the fireplace. He dropped his head on to his paws and settled down to sleep.

'Sorry about the interruption,' Jake said into his computer screen as he sat down in front of it. 'Neighbour trouble.'

His best friend, Will Heath, leaned toward the camera of his own laptop. Behind him the lights of Hollywood twinkled in the Californian evening.

'As you never had problems with Miss South, you must mean that the dastardly Miss Brinkley has moved in next door.

'What's wrong? Did she park her broomstick across your driveway?'

'It's not funny, Will,' Jake growled.

'You're right. It's hilarious!' His friend grinned. 'A new neighbour has had the cheek to move in next door to Hawthorn Ridge's Mr Grumpy. What's she like? Pretty?'

'You never change, Will!'

The question gave Jake time to think, which was a mistake. Miss Brinkley's gaze from chocolate-coloured eyes came back to him. It had been wide eyed until a tendril of hair had blown across her long, dark lashes.

He scowled.

'That bad, eh?' his friend prompted.

'No. I'm trying to remember, that's all.'

Will chuckled. How could he laugh when it came to women?

How could he laugh at all?

'She's just your sort, Will,' Jake said at last.

The glee fled from his friend's face.

'That doesn't sound like you, Jake.'

Will peered out from the screen as though he was trying to look across the miles that separated their transatlantic call.

'No.' Jake's mouth was set.

He didn't want to poke a stick into the embers of the topic they hated discussing.

Some things were better left in silence, even between best friends.

'Come on, out with it. I've never known you to encourage me in any of my little hobbies before, Jake.'

Will had a lot of good qualities, but the only real interests he had in life were having a good time, women and acting. In that order.

'That's because there's no person I'd rather see swept off her feet by you and whisked away to Beverley Hills,' Jake replied. 'I moved into this house because I wanted to take time out from life on the farm. To get some peace and quiet.'

Will pulled a face.

'As it's a woman, she must be opening a beautician's, a spa or a yoga studio. Yes, that'll be it for sure.

'Car doors slamming all day as a stream of gorgeous girls arrive for their sessions. Constant giggling and nattering on the doorstep, the paparazzi . . .'

'In California, maybe. In Hawthorn Ridge?' Jake mocked, but Will was warming to his theme.

'I can hear it now. 'Come along, ladies, downward dog!' drifting through the windows. Which will always be open because they like a nice circulation of air when they exercise. Hmm.

'I was thinking of coming over to visit you soon, Jake. Ask Ms Brinkley if I can attend one of her sessions, will you?'

'It's not going to be a yoga studio, Will. And talking about women like that is definitely not politically correct.'

Will shrugged.

'Then it must be a gym. Even better! Although I can see you wouldn't want to hear pounding treadmills, blaring music, grunting and groaning from six a.m. to eleven at night.'

'She's not opening a gym, either.'

Will's brow wrinkled in thought.

Jake pulled his hand down over his face. For a great bloke Will could be frustrating at times.

'Haven't you anything better to do?

Let's change the subject.'

Will shook his head.

'No. Winding you up is so much fun.'

'She wants to open a nursery.' Jake gave in.

'There's not a lot of room for plants in Miss South's old place, is there?'

'Not that sort of nursery,' Jake snapped. 'She wants to fill the house with kids.'

The laughter vanished from Will's eyes.

'Oh. Like you and Jenny?'

Jake spoke through gritted teeth.

'You were supposed to change the subject, Will.'

His friend's gaze dropped to his keyboard. There was a long silence.

'You know me, Jake,' he muttered eventually. 'I'm guaranteed to put my foot in it somehow.'

Hollywood Star

'Jenny was the world's best wife.' Jake had said those words so often over the past five years that they could find their own way out past the truth.

'The world's best sister, too,' Will added.

You and me and Jenny. The three of us were the perfect proof that opposites attract, Jake replied silently.

He could never say it out loud.

'It might be OK, Jake. Your new neighbour's business might not get any customers. There can't be anybody under fifty living in Hawthorn Ridge apart from you. It's always been Snoozeville Central!

'That's why it was the perfect place for you — although I was surprised when you moved down into the valley.'

'Lack of excitement is exactly why I moved to Plum Tree Cottage. I was cramping Maisey's style.'

'So you moved out of the farm to give

your little sister the run of that huge house? Have you heard what happens when party invitations go viral?'

'That only happens when someone like you is behind the chaos!'

Jake laughed, glad that they'd moved away from the topic of Jenny.

'Maisey is only allowed to have parties when Dylan is home from university. He can keep an eye on things.'

Will's eyes widened.

'Your baby brother is likely to be worse than her! I don't believe that medical students are famously sober and level-headed pillars of the community!'

'Dylan has finals coming up next year. He's determined to pass and he's going for a distinction.'

Will beamed.

'Good for him. I wish I had that sort of focus. I've the attention span of a fruit fly!'

Jake smiled. Will had no illusions about himself. If only he could be more like that.

'Dylan wishes he had your sort of

money, no doubt, Will.'

'Tell him if I can survive until he qualifies, I'll take him on as my private medic.'

'You need patching up again?'

'Blame the person who decided to remake 'This Sporting Life' to appeal to the US market. My character has to play American football rather than rugby league.

'A seventeen-stone defender stopped me like a midge on set today. It was like running into a brick wall!'

'Isn't that what stunt doubles are for?' Jake asked.

Will grunted.

'I thought it would be no different from my days playing team games at school with you. Turns out rugby, like American football, is a young man's game.'

'Thirty-two is not old,' Jake retorted, trying to convince himself as well as Will.

'Prove it. Stop being a misery and throw a welcoming party for your new neighbour.'

'Me? Throw a party?'

'Well, maybe not. Help her settle in.'

'You'll be setting me up with her next!'

'Would I?' Will was all innocence. 'Listen, if you're worried, make her think you've dropped your objections. Then you two can jog along happily unless you have to complain in future.'

Jake imagined pre-schoolers thumping around next door.

'Don't you mean 'when' I have to complain rather than 'unless'?'

'The thing is she'll know it's a genuine grievance because you started off well. That will make her feel guilty.

'Go and ask if she needs help,' Will continued. 'Make her feel welcome. I know you, Jake. You'll raise all sorts of obstacles.

'For once don't man the barricades; break them down. Try to work with her, not against her.'

'Why didn't I think of this?' Jake asked with heavy irony. 'Perhaps I should volunteer to dress up as Father Christmas and hand presents round at the annual children's party!'

They both sat for a while without saying anything.

'Tell you what, let's check our diaries,' Will said at last. 'I know you're only just back from a project, but when was the last time you went away on a proper holiday?'

'You should know,' Jake muttered. 'It was when I took Jenny to Australia. You came along, too. Our third wheel.'

Will rolled his eyes.

'Work with me, man. I'm trying to cheer us both up!'

'OK, well, that'll be seven years ago this November.'

'Then you're overdue a break. My film work wraps up tomorrow, so why not come over and stay with me for a while?

'I can stop you brooding, and you can keep me on the straight and narrow.'

His words helped Jake raise a sliver of a smile.

'There's no way anyone will ever do that!' he argued.

Make a Wish

The Wishing Tree Nursery had been set up in what had once been Hawthorn Ridge's Methodist chapel. On the ground floor was a large hall with kitchen, toilets and small meeting-rooms pretty much unchanged from the building's Victorian heyday.

Elizabeth had developed an upper floor to provide living accommodation. There were two bedrooms, box-room and a bathroom.

Emma had chosen the rear bedroom. It had a view of the tree that gave the nursery its name — a mulberry on a grassy bank that rose up behind the chapel.

When Elizabeth had opened the nursery as a day-care centre many years before, she had encouraged the children to hang little cards on the old tree with their wishes.

A generous woman, she made as many of them come true as she could.

'Not as many as I'd like as time went

on,' she had told Emma. 'When I started out, a trip to the zoo or seaside was a big treat for a lot of the children. I could manage such an outing once or twice a year.

'We had pets, too, so those who couldn't have one at home could enjoy them.

'Then their wish lists started to include things like mobile phones and designer trainers. How could I afford those?

'I couldn't bear to disappoint the children, so the Wishing Tree idea was abandoned.'

Emma thought the story behind the Wishing Tree was lovely but, like Elizabeth, she wouldn't want to disappoint any child.

That didn't mean the poor old tree would be forgotten. On impulse she now took the label from one of her houseplants.

Threading a length of string through the hole in one end, she found an indelible pen and, after some thought, wrote her own wish on the label.

I wish that this nursery is a big success!

Taking the label outside, she went through the overgrown garden, climbed the grassy bank and tied her wish among the autumnal yellow leaves of the old tree.

* * *

Emma unpacked the last of her clothes and put them away in the wardrobe. The old chapel would soon be filled with children again, she was sure.

She thought of a recent chat with her aunt in her new home in Cheltenham.

'Living here means I'm close to everything I need,' Elizabeth had said. 'There's so much more going on here in town. Are you sure life in Hawthorn Ridge will be lively enough for you, Emma?'

Emma had laughed.

'Over the past few months I've had 'lively' up to here!' She put her fingers at her ears.

Her new life in Hawthorn Ridge

seemed to promise the best of both worlds — the lively company of little children all day, then peace after the toddlers went home each evening.

She had a sudden pang. That wasn't the existence she'd dreamed about when Leonard asked her to marry him.

Emma had hoped settling down would give her the family life she'd missed as a child. She had longed for a stable home with two parents who loved each other.

At the heart of all her dreams had been the idea of starting a family.

She should have seen the danger signs. Leonard was full of plans for finishing his studies and then seeing the world. The subject of children never came up.

If they were out together and happened to pass a family, Emma always smiled at them but Leonard never seemed to notice.

The final warning should have been when he discovered a local building society was advertising for staff. Once he pointed out one of the perks was a cut-rate mortgage Emma's fate seemed sealed.

At the time Emma was earning less as a nanny than the building society was offering for an entrance-level position.

Working in finance would let her save more toward their wedding, Leonard suggested. He himself was determined to become an architect.

As a bonus they would be able to start house-hunting much sooner.

Within days Emma had given up a career she loved for a better-paid post that gave her no job satisfaction.

Her relationship with Leonard never recovered. She suspected they should have been talking about things that mattered more than wedding venues and menus.

'I was stupid to assume he felt the same way I did,' Emma scolded herself for the millionth time. 'It was a blessing in disguise Leonard called it off before it was too late.'

It turned out that Leonard was just like her new neighbour when it came to the subject of children.

Emma's mouth twisted in a rueful smile. Here she was, trying to mend her shattered heart by opening a nursery! It would be funny if it weren't so sad.

She hadn't tried to persuade Leonard to change his mind about becoming a father. If his heart wasn't in it both he and their child would have suffered. It would have been cruel.

Her mother had said Leonard was bound to come around to the idea of having a family in the end.

Emma wasn't so sure. Her own father had never warmed to the idea.

He had abandoned her mother while Emma was still a baby. As she was growing up Emma had learned the details of her mother's sad story bit by bit.

She had decided that marriage and, more importantly, family life, had to be a partnership. She also knew that the most successful partnerships, whether in business or in life, needed everyone to be completely honest with each other.

'At least Mr Allen has left me in no doubt about where I stand with him,' she muttered now, frowning at a sudden amount of noise coming from next door.

There was an awful lot of barking going on in Plum Tree Cottage.

That man had a cheek. He complained about all the noise this nursery hadn't started making yet and then he let his dog make that terrible racket!

Emma hoped it wasn't going to carry on all night long.

Intruders

Next morning, Emma went downstairs still half asleep.

Walking into the living-room at the back of the house, she got a shock. The garden outside was full of deer!

Sensing movement inside the house, they cantered away uphill. Jostling into an overgrown corner behind some bushes, they disappeared one by one, then reappeared in the field beyond Emma's garden fence.

With the animals running away towards a nearby copse, Emma felt brave enough to go out and investigate.

She would have to find a shop that sells wellingtons, she thought, picking her way between the nettles and brambles of her overgrown garden.

There was an eight-feet-high fence of wire mesh between the chapel and the field beyond, which should have kept the deer out. She found out what had happened.

A dead bough had fallen and landed on the old fence, weighing it down to the point where even she could have hopped over it easily.

That would need to be fixed right away. Her new garden might be nothing special at the moment, but Emma had big plans. Those deer would graze everything down to the ground in no time!

Emma pulled out her phone to add 'Find fence-mender' under her note to buy wellingtons.

As she tapped away a voice rang out from the direction of Plum Tree Cottage.

'Hello?'

Turning, Emma saw a girl's face peering at her from above the high stone wall separating the two properties.

'Hi! I'm Maisey Allen. Can I have a word? It's Emma, isn't it?'

'Yes, but how do you know my name?' Emma asked, making her way to the wall. 'Sorry I'm only in my dressing-gown!'

'Don't worry. So am I!' The girl waved, showing a lavender towelling sleeve. 'My mum's on the Hawthorn Ridge planning committee.

'She doesn't let out any trade secrets, but the whole village has been waiting to meet Miss Emma Brinkley!'

Emma let out her breath. Unlike Mr J.P. Allen his partner looked friendly.

'Well, here I am. Large as life and twice as natural!' Emma gave a self-deprecating shrug.

She could hear the patter of dog's paws out of sight in the garden next door.

'I want to apologise for Tiger disturbing you, Emma.'

'He hasn't — I've always been an early riser. I came out because I saw deer in my garden.'

'Ah, so that's what started this holy terror barking just now!'

Realisation hit Emma.

'Is that why he was making such a racket last night?'

Maisey was horrified.

'Are you saying he disturbed you then?'

'No, not at all. I was only worried that

something might be wrong with him. I thought he was ill.'

'Tiger? No, he's as fit as a butcher's dog. Or rather a photographer's dog!'

That was another piece of information for Emma to fit into the jigsaw of her new surroundings.

'Your husband is a photographer?' Mr J.P. Allen might be a misery, but it sounded like he had an interesting job.

Emma's mind began to race ahead with the idea of an annual photo session for her nursery's children.

Maisey looked puzzled.

'I'm not married.'

'Oh. Your partner, then. Mr J.P. Allen?'

The girl's face relaxed instantly.

'Jake's nothing like that. He's my brother! If you're going to call him Mr J.P. Allen that will make him laugh!'

That man laugh? Chance would be a fine thing!

Emma looked at Maisey closely. She shared her brother's colouring, but her blue eyes were as soft as the dark hair curling around her face.

'I can see the resemblance,' Emma told her. 'So your mum is on the committee that let my application through while Mr — sorry, Jake — objected to it?

'That must mean your family is at daggers drawn!'

Maisey laughed.

'Quite the opposite. Mum had a job to do and she did it, end of story. I'm sure the two of them never give it a second thought.

'Mind you, Mum is wondering about buying Jake a pair of noise-cancelling headphones for Christmas.'

Emma chuckled.

'Jake is Mum's favourite, anyway,' Maisey went on. 'Probably because he's the complete opposite of our dad.

'For a start Jake won't hear of putting Tiger in kennels when he goes away on business. That's why I'm here today.

'I act as Jake's live-in dog-sitter, then life can go on as normal for Tiger. Trouble is, I went and left a kitchen window open last night, didn't I?'

She rolled her eyes.

'Tiger must have heard those deer mooching down from the woods and he started raising Cain!'

'He went quiet after a few minutes,' Emma remembered.

'Yes, it's amazing what a few dog treats can do.'

'Do deer come round here often? I didn't expect them to be so big and, to be honest, I was a bit scared. I've only ever seen them on TV before. I was glad they ran away.'

She giggled self-consciously.

'You must think I'm a real coward.'

'You'll get used to it,' Maisey replied with easy charm. 'Leave them alone and they'll leave you alone. Although if they're getting in you'll need to check your fence. They'll ruin your garden.'

Emma gazed at the wilderness surrounding the Wishing Tree Nursery.

'They can't do much damage yet. In fact, I'd be happy for them to nibble away at all this horrible undergrowth!'

'Don't bother trying to do anything with the garden until you've had the fence repaired,' Maisey advised. 'Deer will sneak in anywhere.

'I can't say I blame them. If I was an animal I'd much rather eat proper plants than boring old grass.'

'Getting the fence fixed has gone on to my to-do list, don't worry,' Emma replied firmly. 'I was going to look online for a firm of fencers, but you can't always trust reviews on there.

'I'd rather contact a local firm, anyway. Is there a village Facebook page I could check out?'

'Yep, just search for 'Hawthorn Ridge Help'. There's always something needs doing up at our farm, so we employ regular contractors and some freelance workers.

'I'll ask around, too, if you like. I'm sure somebody would be happy to look at the job.

'Make sure you get a few quotes from different people to be on the safe side.'

'Thank you,' Emma replied. 'Wow, I expected country life to be really quiet, but I couldn't have been more wrong!

'I've not only seen deer today, but have also met somebody who actually lives on a farm!' Emma laughed.

'Well, it's Jake, my big brother, who owns Hawthorn Ridge Farm. What do you say to that?' Maisey's blue eyes twinkled with mischief.

'Get off my land!' was what Emma thought Jake Allen would probably like shouting, but she decided not to say so.

'I'm sure he enjoys its wide-open spaces,' she said diplomatically. 'Why does he live in Plum Tree Cottage, then?'

'Ah, well,' Maisey said after a moment. 'There's a long story behind that. You'll learn once you've been properly sucked into village life.

'Have you got a dog?' she asked, peering over the wall to check.

Emma shook her head.

'I've never had the room before.'

'Pity. People with dogs always settle in quickly here. You can find your way around by taking them out for walks. That gives you a good excuse to introduce yourself to people on the way.

'It's why I gave Tiger to Jake. As a distraction after — well, a family tragedy.'

She looked down towards her feet and fell silent.

Emma guessed that Tiger was still there, out of sight on the other side of the wall.

She wanted to hear more about why Jake had moved from his farm to the cottage next door, but Maisey seemed keen to change the subject.

The Hermit

'Everybody expects the first night with a new puppy to be noisy, but Tiger drove Jake mad for nearly a week,' Maisey declared. 'It was trying to find out what made this dog ballistic that brought him back to life.

'Finally he realised it was deer jumping over the low fence that went round Plum Tree Cottage at the time. When they got near the house Tiger could hear them.'

'Exactly what happened last night,' Emma marvelled.

Maisey nodded.

'Jake put in a higher boundary all along the back, including Miss South's garden. Tiger's been good at night ever since.'

Emma shook her head.

'If I had a puppy I'd take the poor little thing upstairs to bed with me long before it could give me all those sleepless nights!'

Maisey was shocked.

'That's the last thing you should do! When you're born and raised on a farm like we were you know that, when it comes to animals, you start as you mean to go on.'

'You've got to treat them like you treat children?' Emma asked. 'I see. Show them the kind of behaviour you want and don't let them take advantage of you.'

'Exactly. How many kids do you have, Emma?'

'None of my own. I'm not married.' The words tumbled out before Emma could stop them.

She went bright red and looked away from Maisey's curious gaze.

'But that's a sore subject at the moment.'

'OK,' the girl said warily. 'Well, you don't need to worry about Jake giving you the third degree. He has too many sore subjects of his own to prod around in anyone else's.

'In any case, he's staying with a friend for a couple of weeks. You might have heard of him. Will Heath, the film star.'

'*The* Will Heath? You're kidding!'

'The very one. They were at school together, then Jake married Will's sister.'

Emma decided this must be one of the topics it was better not to explore. She was curious, but didn't want to pry so soon after her arrival in the village.

'Is your farm very far away?' she asked instead.

Maisey shook her head.

'The field behind these two buildings runs up to Hawthorn Ridge.' She waved at the slope behind the Wishing Tree Nursery. 'Our farm is on the top behind the copse.'

She pointed to a billow of beech trees. Like the Wishing Tree they were already speckled with the shades of autumn.

'Our family has lived there since the year dot, although it's a fair bet that the first one who pitched up there with his stone axe wouldn't recognise his old hunting ground after what we've done to it!'

'Is it so bad?' Emma asked, the picture

of wicked Farmer Jake Allen growing bigger in her mind.

Maisey screwed up her face.

'Grandad was probably the worst. His motto was 'kill everything that doesn't make money'.

'Dad was the complete opposite. He was a bit of a hipster in his youth. He didn't like getting his hands dirty so he let a lot of stuff slide.

'As for Jake, he's keen on what he calls 'maximising streams of income'. He was busy turning the whole farm over to added-value enterprises when he retreated here.

'It does at least mean there are always plenty of people coming and going up at the farm. We rent out business units and storage units and let part of it to a riding stables.

'That was one reason why Jake moved into Plum Tree Cottage. He's not one for socialising. Calls himself the hermit of Hawthorn Ridge.'

'And there was me hoping to make that job description my own!' Emma laughed.

Maisey looked at her askance.

'I thought you were planning to fill the old chapel with screaming kids?' She nodded toward the building. 'That's what Jake based his objection on, anyway.'

Emma sighed.

'You know that saying about what you've never had you never miss? Well, when it comes to children it's not true.'

'Oh.'

Emma gave a rueful smile. Maisey could only be a few years younger than she was, but there was a huge gulf separating them.

She made her explanation short.

'I wanted children, my ex-fiancé didn't. We agreed to disagree.'

Maisey's eyebrows rose.

'Ouch!'

'That's the polite version of what I thought when he called off our wedding six weeks before the big day.'

Maisey's mouth fell open.

'You're kidding!'

'I wish I was.'

'How long ago was this?'

'Eight months, three weeks and two days ago. Not that I'm counting!'

Something close to relief crossed Maisey's face.

'Not long, then. So you haven't moved into Hawthorn Ridge in search of Mr Right?'

It was Emma's turn to be thunder-struck.

'You have got to be joking! As far as I'm concerned, from now on all males are Mr Wrong, not Mr Right.'

'Hear that, Tiger?' Maisey looked down toward the dog again. 'Our Jake is going to be quite safe with Emma.'

'From the way your brother looked at me when I introduced myself he doesn't consider himself to be in any danger!'

'Don't worry; Jake's harmless. At least I think he is.' She looked at Emma side-ways.

Whether he was or not, Jake Allen wouldn't be getting the better of her, Emma thought.

Over the past two years her eyes had

been opened to how much trouble men could be. That was why she had been so keen to move away from everything familiar and make this fresh start.

After what she had been through she wouldn't allow anyone to make her life a misery ever again.

A Fruitful Exchange

'Are you sure you won't stay for another week?' Will asked as Jake lifted a steak from the barbecue and dropped it on to his friend's plate. 'I'll miss your cooking!'

'Maria won't miss all the extra washing-up I create.' Jake nodded appreciatively to his friend's housekeeper as she added the sides of coleslaw, fries and salad.

Maria bustled over to put the plate on the table beside Will's lounger. Not even Jake's cooking could tempt his friend away from the side of the pool in weather like this.

Before picking up his plate, Will paused and scanned the Hollywood hills.

'Jen would have loved it here, wouldn't she?'

It was moments like this when Jake could console himself that every cloud really did have a silver lining. When Will talked about Jenny he always pitched on topics that brought back memories of

Jake's marriage to his sister.

They acted as an antidote somehow to Jake's own sad thoughts of his loss.

'Definitely. It's a shame Jen never got to see you make it big in films.'

'And wouldn't she have just loved Rodeo Drive?' Will set about cutting his steak into bite-sized chunks.

'I would never have been able to tear her away from the shops.'

'You two really did prove that opposites attract.' Will took a sip of his beer.

After such a statement Jake always kept quiet. Will ought to be allowed to keep his treasured memories.

* * *

Tiger lay dozing, shaded from the September sunshine by the old plum tree that gave Jake's cottage its name.

Emma was busy picking the last of its fruit. Every so often she winced as her palm throbbed with pain.

A few minutes before she had closed her fingers over a wasp. The insect had been on the opposite side of one ripe plum and had reacted by giving her a sharp sting.

When Tiger sprang to his feet with a whimper, Emma guessed what was wrong.

'Don't tell me, Tiger. You've been stung!'

The dog took no notice of her. His ears were pricked toward a different sound.

Trotting down the path to the garden gate, he stuck his nose between its bars and started to whine.

The road outside looked deserted. Emma picked up her basket of plums and followed the dog. There must be something going on further up the valley.

As she reached the garden gate, a taxi swept into view and pulled into the kerb right in front of her.

Tiger started dancing with delight as the door was thrown open.

Emma saw Jake Allen.

Stepping out of the cab he stopped and stared. The look on his face told Emma the sight of her in his garden, carrying a basket of fruit, was the last thing he expected to see.

'What the — ?'

'Maisey said I could have as many of these plums as I liked since you wouldn't want them,' she said defensively.

It wasn't strictly true.

'My stupid brother will only leave them to rot,' had been Maisey's exact words.

Emma thought it was safer to tone the message down.

'OK,' he said slowly as he settled the taxi fare.

After unloading his luggage, he opened the gate then reached down to make a fuss of his dog.

'First things first. Although some guard dog you are, Tiger!'

As she couldn't see his expression Emma wasn't sure whether Jake was being funny or not.

'I feel awkward now that I didn't wait until you got home, Mr — Jake,' she corrected herself quickly. 'The trouble was nobody knew how long you were likely to be away.

'I'm sorry if you feel I should have waited. I couldn't bear to see all this lovely fruit going to waste.'

Jake still seemed more interested in Tiger than in the loss of his fruit. She took that to be a good sign.

'Maisey told me you usually let your mother have the plums and, with Mrs Allen having moved out of the farm, she hasn't got the time or the room to make jam any more.'

'It's a pity Maisey never asked me about it first,' Jake replied.

His voice had the sound of being strained through tight lips.

'It just so happens I was going to try using some of the fruit myself this year. I've brought a recipe back from America.'

Emma wondered if he was telling the truth. Jake Allen didn't look like the sort of man who would eat quiche, let alone list cooking among his hobbies.

Maybe he was only saying this to be

awkward and to put her firmly in the wrong.

'What recipe is that?' she asked casually, trying to catch him out. 'I'm always keen to try new ones.'

'Plum salsa.'

He gave the reply so easily that Emma decided to give him the benefit of the doubt.

'Have these back.' She held her basket out toward him. 'There are more in my kitchen, too. This is my second basketful.

'I'm all set to make jam, chutney, and fruit juice, but I was beginning to wonder what to do with it all. I thought I'd have to buy a lot more sugar, jars, and bottles.'

He looked at her sharply.

'Don't you recycle the same ones every year? That's what my mother does.'

'Of course I do. The trouble is I give lots of things away as presents and not everyone returns the jars.

'By the way, I was going to let you have as much as you like since it's being made with fruit from your tree.'

He almost smiled.

'I'll look forward to that.'

It was on the tip of Emma's tongue to ask him for the salsa recipe he had mentioned, but she took too long gathering courage.

He was already pulling his luggage into the garden, ready to pass her.

'Well, if you'll excuse me I've been travelling for fifteen hours and I've some jet lag to deal with.

'And you have all those plums to cook.'

He looked down at the glittering fruit lying in the basket on her arm. A Red Admiral landed on one of them and began tasting its bloom.

'Let me know how many you'll need for your salsa and I'll put them on the top of the wall outside my kitchen door. They'll be safe enough there,' Emma promised. 'I wouldn't want to disturb you by knocking in case you're sleeping off that jet lag.'

'Good idea. Thanks.'

Was there a faint thawing in his

grumpy exterior? Emma watched him bend to tease a grass seed from the fur beside his dog's ear.

'I'll place a note of what I need there as soon as I've checked the recipe. Come on, Tiger.'

Tiger had forgotten all about his new friend Emma. He only had eyes for Jake.

He trotted along at his master's heels as the pair made their way toward the house. Neither gave her a backward glance.

Emma watched them go, then carried her latest hoard of edible treasure back home.

Peace Offering

Emma stood back to survey her handiwork. The kitchen table was half covered with jars of freshly made jam, waiting to be labelled.

The kitchen was hot. A tiny breeze whispered through the room as Emma wrote out labels for her preserves.

She had decided to give her neighbour some, to show what she'd done. She could ask him for the salsa recipe, too.

She stuck labels on two jars, making sure they were perfect in every way. Jake Allen was sure to be a stickler for details.

After packing the bottles into a small cardboard box, she carried it to his front door and pressed the bell. Tiger barked, galloping around the side of the house to meet her.

It took Jake a while to open the door.

'Oh, it's you!' he said and disappeared again.

Assuming that was all the welcome

she was going to get, Emma put the box down on his front step and started off home.

Tiger milled around her, wagging his tail. His owner might be rude but Emma couldn't resist making a fuss of the dog.

She was still bending over him when Jake returned to open the front door fully.

'I'm glad I caught you,' he said.

'You could have fooled me. It looked like you were running away!'

'Sorry, I was tied up with something. Here, I've printed out the salsa recipe for you, plus something else you might need.'

He handed her a sheaf of papers.

'You could have done with these before you started work on the plums.'

'Thank you for the recipe,' Emma said with cold dignity, 'but I can't imagine what else I could possibly need from you.'

'That's what I hoped you'd say.' He nodded gravely and stepped back inside

Tiger pattered indoors behind him.

'That told him!' Emma muttered as he closed the door.

Then she saw what Jake had given her — two sheets of small adhesive labels, just the right size for sticking on jars of preserves. Each bore a motto.

Please wash and return to Emma Brinkley.

These were exactly what she needed. Who would have thought the hermit of Hawthorn Ridge would think of it?

Jake's salsa recipe was good. Emma made a small batch and had some with her lunch. She felt guilty. She ought to go round and apologise for being so sniffy with him. Once she had made a big batch of plum chutney she took a couple of jars to him.

'A peace offering,' she announced before he could get the door fully open. 'I was rude to you. I've brought you some chutney to make up for it.

'Thanks for those labels. Look, I've stuck them on the bottom of these two jars.'

'Why would I need them?' he huffed.

'Ah-ah-ah!' Emma wagged her finger with mock severity. 'They aren't for you, but for when you're away.

'If Maisey is doing the washing-up here and she comes across an empty jar she'll know not to stick it in the recycling.'

His tense features relaxed into a smile.

'Good point. I'm glad you mentioned my sister. Have you done anything about recruiting staff for your nursery? She might be looking for a job.'

Emma bit her lip. It was difficult enough living next door to someone who didn't share her vision for the future.

What if she employed his sister and Maisey turned out to be no good?

'I'm still looking round,' she replied carefully. 'I'll need qualified staff as the Wishing Tree is for pre-schoolers. I've started casting round online.'

'Have you found anyone yet?'

For a man who had been so opposed to her plans Jake seemed very interested in how she was getting on.

Emma wondered if he was gathering

information for another attack.

She decided to play it cool.

'I've a few candidates lined up. The council is coming this week to do some final checks before I open for business. I plan to fit interviews around that.'

'In that case I'm sure Maisey would be interested in applying. She's always wanted to work with children and she's been earning money as a babysitter since she was fourteen.'

Emma's heart sank. The sister of her enemy and a keen amateur? It sounded like a recipe for disaster.

Jake went on.

'She was set to go to Norland College.'

Emma was suddenly much more interested.

'Where Royal nannies are trained?'

Jake looked uneasy and it was a few seconds before he went on.

'Before she could take up her place there the farm hit a sticky patch. Everybody's plans had to go on hold. The business had to diversify or close.

'Among other things I leased some of

the buildings to a riding stables. Maisey has been brought up with horses. With no commuting or other fees, working there was an obvious move for her.

'She started earning rather than running up student debt. She's fully CRB checked and has got all the relevant first-aid certificates, too.'

Emma did like Maisey and could see the pair of them working well together.

'It sounds as though I should see her,' she began slowly. 'One thing does worry me about you volunteering her for a job, Jake. If Maisey is such a perfect candidate, why has she never said anything to me when we've been chatting?'

'You can blame me for that.' Jake looked suitably apologetic. 'Maisey is convinced I've been making your life a misery. She must think you look on us Allens with suspicion and you'd never employ her.

'On top of that I was the one who put a stop to her original career plans. It's a very sore point between us.

'We never talk about it or else I would

have suggested she asked you herself.'

He looked embarrassed.

'Ah, well, you know what they say. You can choose your friends, but you can't choose your relatives. The poor girl can't help being your sister.'

Emma gave him a playful nudge.

'Of course I'll see her! Get her to put all her qualifications, relevant experience and why she'd want a job into an e-mail. I'll take it from there.'

'Thanks, Emma.' He looked relieved.

'Don't mention it. In fact, you might be able to help me in return. Can you think of anywhere else I could look for qualified staff?'

'Sorry, no. At the farm we've used the same firms of contractors since dinosaurs roamed the earth. I've never had cause to investigate employment agencies.

'I could ask around among the staff, though. Loads of them have kids so they might know the best place to look for help.

'When I was in the market for that kind

of thing, I knew the local clinic and the council held lists of registered childminders. I'm pretty sure they work through the internet now, though.'

Emma couldn't help wondering when and why child-hating Jake Allen would have been 'in the market for that kind of thing'.

In that moment, she decided to look him up online. Everyone left a trail on the internet, after all, and there were limits to what she could ask his sister.

Especially when Maisey might become an employee.

Good Advice

'Don't take this the wrong way, Emma, but how are your finances?'

The unexpected question brought her back to earth with a bump.

'What a thing to ask!'

He raised his hand in a calming gesture.

'Sorry. I'm only trying to help. As one business person to another.'

Emma tried to settle her ruffled feelings. The matter of money was a sensitive one, to be honest.

It was made worse by the thought that her neighbour appeared pretty well-off, with his farm diversity schemes and his house here in the village.

'As a matter of fact, my aunt is helping me out with that,' she replied. 'She paid for all the updating that's been done and she's letting me live here rent free for a trial period.

'The place needed renovating so she's persuaded me I'm doing her a favour.'

Jake nodded in agreement.

'She's right — an occupied house is less likely to be burgled. Keeping the building warm will prevent it deteriorating over the winter, too.

'You'll also be on the spot in case of any accidents. Last December pipes burst in a house further up the valley. As it was a holiday let water kept pouring out from under the front door for days before I managed to get in contact with the owners. Their garden was a skating rink!'

'It sounds like country people have a lot to put up with.' Emma sighed.

Jake laughed without humour.

'This is Hawthorn Ridge. There's only one thing the locals like less than incomers and that's absentee landlords.

'I'm afraid it might have been the thought of the owners' faces, when they arrived at the Nook in spring to find it sodden and mouldy, that stopped anyone getting in touch with them.'

His jaw was set in a disapproving line.

'That doesn't give the local people

much credit!' she protested.

Would Emma have to get on the right side of every local person she met?

'I know. I can say that because I'm a local myself,' Jake replied grimly.

'It sounds like I'll have to be very careful when it comes to advertising my business.'

Emma grazed her lower lip with her teeth, 'The mums who use the Thursday drop-in sessions here are great. Their word-of-mouth recommendations will sell this place better than anything else.

'But I need to advertise the Wishing Tree Nursery in as many other places as I can think of. How am I to do that without offending anybody?

'I can put out the word online, obviously,' she went on. 'The primary school and the village shop both have noticeboards, so they are obvious places to put up adverts.

'I was thinking of doing a leaflet drop, too.'

Jake looked doubtful.

'You'll need to be very careful. The

junk-mail plague has eased off round here but people still moan about it. You don't want to annoy anyone before you start.

'Try to target only households with children — places where you see toys in the garden, small clothes on the line. That sort of thing.'

'Good idea.'

Jake was turning out to be far more than just a pretty face.

'Jake, have you had anything to do with Carey's Cleansing?' Emma asked. 'I was going to contact them to see if they would advertise the Wishing Tree among their staff.'

Jake inhaled deeply.

'Anyone living here has had dealings with Mr Carey one way or another.'

Emma started making notes on her phone.

'Right, so what do I need to know about him?'

Jake was silent for so long that Emma looked up to prompt him.

He was staring at some distant point

above her head.

Sensing her movement, he dropped his gaze and frowned.

'Colin Carey is a person I'm careful not to think too much about. When you are in business you have to deal with all sorts of people, unfortunately.'

'I thought you were a photographer. That's art, not business.'

Jake raised his eyebrows so high they almost reached his hairline.

'You've heard that old line about artists starving in a garret? That's because they don't understand how business works. There's a big difference between pleasing yourself and earning a living.'

He considered his next words carefully, before taking direct action.

Stepping back, he invited her into his house.

'Come with me.'

Confessions

While Jake closed the door behind her Emma admired the art prints of fruits and flowers set out along the hallway walls.

'Did you take these photographs?' she asked as he directed her to the kitchen.

'Took them, developed them and framed them. It's what I do — when I'm not covering wars around the world.'

He opened a door leading out into the garden and ushered her toward a large home office.

'Ah.' Emma smiled. 'That scuppers my idea of you becoming the Wishing Tree's official child photographer.'

He looked at her quickly.

'Photographing children is a particular form of torture. It needs endless patience — and wipe-clean surfaces!'

'Yes, I'm used to all that!'

'I'd like to spend more time doing art photography and less covering human stories. That's not likely to happen, though.

'We need to try to persuade people how terrible war is and encourage them to help the victims of natural disasters.'

Beneath its green roof, the soft shades of Jake's wood-panelled home office merged with the flowers of late summer.

Jake told Tiger to lie down on the grass then unlocked the door.

'This is my photographic studio.' He stepped aside to let Emma go in first.

Ranged around the shelves were various sizes of lights, reflectors, frames and all kinds of specialist equipment.

What caught Emma's eye was a beautiful print of ripe peaches. They had been photographed growing against the warm red brick of an old wall.

The picture was on a central table. She bent over, fascinated by its subtle colours and textural qualities. Jake's photo had captured the soft fuzziness of the fruit so perfectly they looked good enough to eat.

'This is the next one to go up on your wall?'

'Eventually. I'm holding an exhibition

next year. That's what I mean about creative people needing to keep an eye on business.

'If I can make a success out of autochromes I won't need to go away to photograph disasters so often.'

'Autochromes?'

'An early form of colour photography. Based on potato starch, believe it or not. The images are created on big, heavy glass plates.

'They aren't permanent. Daylight bleaches them quite quickly. The Victoria and Albert Museum has a collection dating back to the late nineteenth century, all stored in light-tight conditions.

'Autochrome fell out of favour a long time ago. These days it's only done by a few enthusiasts.

'I like the effects it can produce, although of course it's all trickery. Those starch grains only come in either blue, red or green,' Jake explained. 'They are so tiny that every shade you see is created by your eye being fooled by combinations of those three colours.'

'If they have to be kept in the dark, how come you've got them hanging along your hallway and I'm looking at this one here?'

'That's the clever part,' he told her. 'Once I've fixed the image on a glass plate using the autochrome technique I can digitise the result. What you're looking at is actually a photograph of a photograph.'

'That is clever.' Emma shook her head in wonder. 'I'll stick to my phone's camera. It's a lot less complicated. And quicker!'

Jake agreed.

'I don't blame you. This was just my hobby. Then a few people got to know what I was doing and wanted copies of my pictures for themselves.

'One thing led to another, so I'm putting on an exhibition in London next year. If there are enough people willing to pay for this type of art then I'm in business.

'If not it'll still be my hobby. Either way I'm happy.'

He ran his hand lovingly over an impressive piece of photographic equipment. It looked seriously expensive.

'I got interested in this while I was at college,' he went on.

'You went to college?' Emma asked. 'I thought you owned a farm.'

'That was back when my father was still alive, before I had to take over. Colleges don't care where you live as long as their fees are paid and you are willing to work.'

Jake obviously had talent. Emma gazed at the beautiful picture on the table and wondered if it was for sale. She ached to ask but held back.

'Was going to college why you moved out of the farm and came to live in Plum Tree Cottage?'

He narrowed his eyes.

'That's a stretch! What do you mean?'

Emma took a chance.

'Maisey told me you'd had trouble at home. Did your father want you to follow the family tradition and become a farmer but you wanted to go to art college?'

'Not quite. It was Dad who suggested I kept up my interest in art while I was at Cirencester Agricultural College.

'He thought it would be a good idea to have a release from the cut and thrust of farming life.'

Emma laughed. Jake didn't.

'Turns out that my father couldn't have been more right.

'With the cost of stock, feed and fertilisers going through the roof, markets contracting and global warming . . . Well, if a farmer doesn't have a watertight business plan they might as well lodge with a starving artist in one of those garrets.

'We diversified up at the farm and eventually I went off to become a photographer. Now my work helps to pay the farm bills.'

'If that's the case, then maybe Maisey should get the chance to follow her own dream,' Emma said quietly.

If Jake's sister wanted an interview

she would get one. Emma had always intended to offer one place on the nursery staff to a local trainee. Maisey would get that position — if she showed promise.

Jake's brows contracted.

'Dad and I argued often enough, but he said a lot of things worth hearing. One of them was that one should only employ the best person for the job.'

Emma stared at him.

'I was just thinking that myself!'

'Why not? It's sound business sense. That's why I wouldn't want you to feel obliged to take Maisey on.

'I'd never hold it against you if you didn't, because I have no idea if she'll be any good. All I know is I'm the reason she lost out on the career she wanted.'

'I'll have to look you up online,' Emma confessed. 'Photographer, businessman, farmer, friend of Will Heath . . .'

He snorted.

'Take my advice and don't bother. All that will tell you is that I've won a clutch of media awards and have never had a successful relationship in my life.'

'All right, I won't,' Emma promised.

'My father was right again when he said no good would come of me marrying Will's sister. These days, when people say their partner is their best friend it makes me wonder.

'Will was and is my closest mate, but sometimes he drives me up the wall. He's a great bloke and we get on well together. We complement each other, I suppose.

'Will would be the first to say he's got a butterfly mind and has trouble seeing things through to the end.'

It had been such a relief to unburden herself to her aunt about her break-up with Leonard that Emma knew she should let Jake talk right now. A listening ear might help him.

'I don't ever remember seeing your friend Will with the same woman twice when he's been photographed at things like the Oscars,' she prompted carefully.

'It turns out Jenny was very like her brother. She and I were polar opposites.'

Jake held her gaze for long moments before breaking away to push his fingers through his hair.

'Why am I telling you this? I've never told anybody else, not even Will. Unless Jenny told him any details, he knew nothing of our problems.

'It's true what they say. Nobody really knows what goes on inside a marriage apart from the two people involved.'

'Then stop,' Emma urged quietly. 'I don't need to know any of it and you don't need to tell me anything.'

Jake nodded.

'Yes, you're right, of course. I'm sorry.'

Emma shook her head.

'Don't be. Let's change the subject. Tell me about your work.'

He closed his eyes for a few seconds to compose himself.

'At first photography was the way I earned my living. Later it became an escape.

'Can you imagine that? Anybody who willingly enters a theatre of war and can't make a positive contribution to the outcome needs their head examined.'

He seemed on firmer ground now he was talking about his work.

'That's why I want to create a book of my artwork. Living in the same place as generations of my ancestors inspires me.

'I've got Tiger now, too, and it's not fair to keep abandoning him. It's becoming easier and easier to use him as an excuse to stay at home.'

'Was that part of Maisey's plan?'

Jake gave her a knowing look.

'She gave me Tiger and he gave me something to focus on when everything was bleak. At first he was my only reason for getting up in the morning.

'Now he's a lot more than that. If you go out and about with a dog around here, people soon strike up a conversation.'

He bent down and tugged Tiger's ear.

'This dog was my passport back into working life. Then I discovered how much I enjoyed the peace and quiet of life here in Hawthorn Ridge.'

Carey's Cleansing

With the nursery all ready to open and jobs advertised online and around the village, Emma's next task was to set about finding customers.

Using her computer, she designed and printed plenty of colourful handouts.

She gave some to each of the little families who came to the Thursday drop-in sessions. They promised to spread the word and give their neighbours handouts as well.

Emma pinned some on the village noticeboard, in the shop, the church and the social club. She wrote a post for the village Facebook site then tackled local businesses.

There was a small industrial estate down by the river. Visiting each unit in turn, Emma left some Wishing Tree Nursery leaflets with them.

Then she approached the biggest employer in the area.

Carey's Cleansing employed domestic

staff to clean offices and homes across a wide local area.

They would tackle anything, using cleaners employed by the hour.

All these workers would need childcare and Emma wanted them to choose the Wishing Tree Nursery.

She was determined to give them a great service, but that wasn't her only reason for making a special appointment with managing director Colin Carey.

What happened after she was shown into his office came as a shock.

'Well, hello, there! What can I do you for?'

Round, rosy-cheeked Colin Carey swerved out from behind his desk.

He crossed the thick carpet toward her, oozing insincerity from every pore.

Emma was almost overpowered by the fumes of his aftershave.

He extended his hand to her.

She shook it, then wished she hadn't. His pink pudgy skin was moist and he gripped her fingers like a strangler vine.

Showing her to his softly upholstered

visitor's chair, Colin perched on the corner of his desk. He was very close to her and his smile was charming.

Emma was not impressed. One of the first things she had noticed when walking into his office was the family photograph on a shelf behind his desk.

He was blocking her view of it at this moment, although that might have been accidental.

When she glanced at his wedding ring, however, the way he thrust his hand into his pocket was not.

'I'm Emma Brinkley. I'm starting up the Wishing Tree Nursery again.

'As you are the biggest employer in the village I thought you might be interested in some kind of reciprocal arrangement, Mr Carey.'

She wished she had chosen her words more carefully. A suggestive smile crawled across his face.

'Ah. So you'll scratch my back if I scratch yours?' he replied, leaning forward.

Emma's hand went protectively to the

small silver pendant at her neck.

She thanked her lucky stars she was wearing a polo-necked jumper and trousers. Any woman who wore a low neckline or short skirt in this man's office would be in trouble.

'What I meant, Mr Carey, is that if enough of your staff wanted to enrol their children at my nursery perhaps we could work out some sort of discount.'

He nodded, seeming to approve of her idea.

'Mates' rates?' he murmured.

Emma decided to make her escape.

She stood up but couldn't resist pushing her luck.

'I'll leave these flyers with you,' she said, edging around him to place a pile of them on the far corner of his desk. 'There are plenty there.

'Perhaps your staff could drop some off at the offices they visit, too?' she asked with a winning smile.

'As long as Mr Brinkley doesn't mind you and me doing business together.' Colin Carey sniggered.

His smile reminded Emma of a slug stretching out across a pane of glass, she thought, trying not to cringe.

It deserved to be wiped clean off his face, in her opinion.

'Not at all. Mr Brinkley is fine with it as long as I earn enough to keep him in raw steak,' she told the horrible man.

She checked her watch.

'Look at the time! I'd better get back to him. He gets angry if men give me any trouble.'

Ducking out from beneath Colin Carey's gaze, Emma left the office with as much dignity as she could manage.

Interviews

Once back home, Emma didn't stop at her own gate. She marched up the path of Plum Tree Cottage and hammered on Jake's door.

'You could have told me that man was a louse!' she cried, hardly giving Jake time to open his door.

He stared at her in astonishment.

'What? I didn't know he was one! I do know he pays his staff minimum wage, plus I've seen him park on pavements and drop litter.

'I've also heard him trying to explain away his dog worrying sheep by saying it was only playing.

'I don't like the man, but I assumed you'd have better luck,' Jake explained. 'After all, you were offering him a good business proposition and starting with a clean sheet.

'It wasn't my place to bad-mouth the guy before you'd had a chance to speak to him.'

Emma thought of what had happened in that office and what Colin Carey had been like.

She bristled with anger.

'He made it clear that there was only one kind of proposition he was really interested in — and it wasn't business.'

'Oh!' Jake frowned. 'Are you OK?'

'Yes.'

She blushed with annoyance at the memory of her close encounter with Colin Carey.

'He's more a pantomime seducer than the real thing, I think. A ladykiller in his own mind but a paper tiger in real life.' She gave a huff of indignation. 'He had the nerve to ask me if there was a Mr Brinkley!'

'I hope you told him there was and that he's over six feet tall and weighs in at sixteen stone!'

'Not in so many words.'

Emma giggled, but Jake was still looking serious.

'Do you want me to go round there and tell him?' he offered.

'It's not obligatory for a man to play the hero, Jake, any more than women ought to sit back and expect to be rescued.

'After what I've been through over the past ten months I feel like stealing your title of local hermit.'

He studied her face.

'Was it that bad before you moved here?'

'In the grand scheme of things, no, I don't suppose it was. My fiancé didn't cheat on me, or lie or steal — at least as far as I know.

'He and I had what the divorce courts call irreconcilable differences. He ended up dumping me a few weeks before our wedding.'

'That's rotten,' Jake agreed.

'I suppose there was one good thing about the whole awful business.' Emma sighed. 'We had the final bust-up before we got married, rather than after.'

He nodded.

'It sounds to me like you had a lucky escape.'

She shot him a pained look.

'It didn't feel like that at the time, I can assure you.'

'Sorry, that was insensitive. How long ago did all this happen?'

'Just before Christmas.'

'Your wounds must still be raw, then.'

Emma looked at him guardedly.

'People don't usually say that. It's more, 'Come on, buck up. Nine months is long enough to produce a baby!''

She wished she hadn't used that particular example. After all, that was the rock on which her relationship with Leonard foundered.

'Spring had hardly sprung before my friends were telling me to move on,' she confided.

'People mean well.' Jake sighed. 'Some try to jolly you out of it, while others say nothing and cross the road to avoid you.

'Quite honestly I don't know which is worse.'

The anguish on his face was impossible to avoid.

Emma had kept her word and not

looked him up online, but one thing was obvious. However terrible her own experience, it was nothing compared with what Jake had been through.

'Well, I've done what they all suggested and have drawn a line under it,' she said, beginning to back off down the path. 'Now it's time to get my fresh start moving. I've interviews to arrange.

'See you around, Jake!'

* * *

Emma interviewed 10 people for jobs at the nursery. Only a couple were completely unsuitable; the other eight had various strengths and no obvious weaknesses.

The choice was difficult. In the end she selected Pam, a fully qualified nursery nurse, with Maisey, who would be a student under training.

Pam and Maisey would be working with the children full time while Emma helped out and dealt with the administration.

Emma planned to start small and build up numbers at the Wishing Tree Nursery gradually.

With all the decorating done and the health and safety training completed, she organised an open weekend.

She designed a display board for the reception area of the nursery and had it professionally painted by a local artist.

The story of the nursery was written underneath a picture of the Wishing Tree, which matched the sign outside the building.

Each letter of the name Wishing Tree was printed on a different-coloured balloon. Pictures of babies and small children playing on the grass beneath a big old tree gave the sign a happy, friendly look.

The advertisements Emma had pinned up and handed out around the village had done the trick. Lots of families came for a look around on the nursery's open day.

They all loved the story.

By the end of that afternoon Emma

had signed up almost as many children as her small staff could cope with.

Opening Day

On the last Monday in October, the Wishing Tree Nursery opened its doors for the first time.

Emma had been so excited that it had taken her ages to get to sleep the night before.

She was awake again before dawn. Trying to get back to sleep was hopeless as she was scared she would oversleep.

There was nothing for it but to get up and keep busy until everyone arrived.

Emma had decided to open the nursery at seven-thirty each morning. That meant younger children could be dropped off before their older siblings were due at the local primary school's breakfast club.

At seven she went out to buy milk from the village shop. When she got back 10 minutes later, a frail auburn-haired woman with a buggy was waiting under the security light outside the nursery.

She introduced herself as Manda

Donovan.

'This is Jesse.' She pulled a little boy out from behind her. 'The baby's Casey,'

Emma bent over the buggy to admire the sleeping baby inside.

'Lovely to meet you, Mrs Donovan, and you, Jesse!'

The little boy gazed at her with grave eyes.

'I don't recognise your name from my list. Did you come to the open day?'

'No,' Mrs Donovan muttered. 'We couldn't make it.'

'No problem! There's plenty of time for you to sign up before we open.

'If you want to come in and have a look at our toys, Jesse, your mum can have a cup of tea and tell me all about you.'

'Sorry, I can't stop.' Mrs Donovan moved the buggy towards Emma. 'It's my first day in a new job.

'I'm supposed to be there by seven-thirty at the latest to catch a minibus. If it goes without me, I'll be sunk.'

Dropping a kiss on Jesse's ginger hair, she shouldered her handbag and made to leave.

'But I need you to fill in registration forms, Mrs Donovan!'

'I can't be late. I'll get the sack!'

'I can't take charge of your children without any details, Mrs Donovan!' Emma called after her.

With a wail, Jesse darted after his mother. Emma had to make a grab for his hand.

'Our address is Number Four, Weavers Cottages,' Mrs Donovan called over her shoulder.

'What about phone numbers in case we need to contact you? Do Jesse and Casey have any allergies? Food likes and dislikes?'

'I'm working at Carey's Cleansing. If you need me you'll have to speak to them. My shift ends at four!' Mrs Donovan shouted back, gathering speed.

'Mama!' Jesse cried.

Emma picked up the little boy and caught hold of one of his hands.

'Wave bye-bye to Mummy, Jesse!'

That was her first mistake. The little

boy burst into tears.

Within seconds a wet feeling down the arm supporting Jesse revealed another problem.

Putting him down, she tried to stem his uncontrollable sobs.

'Let's find your change of clothes.'

With her spare hand she pushed the buggy to the bottom of the steps leading up to the nursery door. There she put Jesse down so she could check what Mrs Donovan had provided for the day.

The buggy contained one baby . . . and that was it. There was no drink, snack or change of clothes for Jesse. No milk nor nappies for the baby, either. There wasn't even a trainer cup or baby bottle!

Emma kneeled down beside the little boy. Like his mother he was thin and pale, with dark circles under his eyes.

'It's a good job we're ready for any emergency here, Jesse! Let's go and raid the spare clothes cupboard.

'Once you're cleaned up you can help me find nappies, formula and a bottle for Casey. We'll have it all ready for when she wakes up.'

The baby was still asleep 20 minutes later when Maisey arrived for work.

Emma led Jesse by the hand to the door to meet her.

'A customer already! Hello, young sir.' Maisey kneeled down beside the little boy.

'Maisey, this is Jesse Donovan. Say hello, Jesse.'

Jesse stared at her in silence.

'Do you live in Weavers Cottages, Jesse?' Maisey asked.

All he did was blink, so Emma had to answer for him.

'Yes, he does. I'm guessing he's around two and a half. His sister looks to be around three months.

'Now you're as wise as me — their mum dashed off to work without filling in any registration forms.'

Maisey pulled a face.

'It's a wonder that poor woman managed to escape from home. I know her husband,' she mouthed over Jesse's head. 'He's notorious. Spends all his spare time at the social club.

'It's a wonder he unchains his wife from the kitchen sink long enough for her to go shopping. I didn't know he had children.'

'Jesse's mum is starting work today at Carey's. We were in the baby room with his sister when we heard you arrive.'

'Oh, great! I'll go and check her out. I love babies!'

'She's still fast asleep by the sound of it.' Emma tapped the baby monitor clipped to her waist.

Pam, the nursery nurse, was next to arrive, followed by twins Darryl and Tyne.

Once their dad had handed their completed registration forms over, Pam held out her hand to Jesse.

'I'm taking Darryl and Tyne to find some toys, Jesse. Why don't you come with us?'

The little boy clung on to Emma's hand and shrank in against her skirt.

'We'll come see you and the boys later,' Emma said. 'It looks like Jesse is going to help me say hello to Madeleine now.'

The clock in reception was saying 7.45 and a plump, flushed woman in business clothes was in the doorway with a little girl with big blue eyes and a cloud of blonde ringlets.

She was dressed in a red corduroy coat with gold fringing, black tights and black, patent leather shoes.

'Hello.'

The little girl's mum handed over her paperwork. She gave her daughter a hug and a kiss then smiled at Emma.

'Have fun!'

Emma thought she must be talking to her daughter. Within seconds she began to wonder . . .

'My name is Madeleine. I'm nearly four and I'm going to school soon. I can spell. M-a-d-e-l-e-i-n-e. See?

'What's your name?'

'I'm Emma, Madeleine, and this is —'

Madeleine wasn't interested. Like a queen moving down a presentation line she had already turned her attention to Jesse.

'What's your name, little boy?' she demanded.

Jesse stared at her.

Madeleine looked up at Emma.

'What's his name?'

'This is Jesse,' Emma began, but Madeleine's mind was now on other things.

'We're going to play 'Repair Shop',' she announced to Jesse and caught his arm.

The little boy's mouth fell open with shock.

'I'm Susie. You have to find something for me to mend,' Madeleine went on.

She then switched her attention back to Emma.

'Where are the toys?'

'I'll show you. We've got a workbench in our playroom that you'll love, Susie.'

Madeleine looked up at Emma with a cold stare.

'You're not in our game. You have to call me Madeleine.'

'Of course, Madeleine,' Emma said gravely, waiting for Jesse to burst into tears again.

His morning, after all, had been full of loss and frightening new experiences.

She braced herself.

Madeleine's tone must have reeled Jesse in from the terrifying sea of his new experiences.

He let go of Emma's hand and looked up at her with an angelic smile and told her to go away with a curse word she had never heard from a child before.

Emma goggled at him, lost for words.

Somehow she managed to keep smiling as she guided the two children into the playroom.

But she couldn't help wondering if she looked as white as she felt.

That afternoon, Emma warned each parent to brace themselves for some bad language, apologising in advance.

She also explained to Jesse's mother what had happened, asked her to persuade Jesse not to swear and gave her admission forms to fill in for her children.

The next morning, Emma waited for

a torrent of complaints from parents whose little angels had developed potty mouths. Luckily there were none.

That wasn't the only thing that didn't happen, however.

'Have you got your admission forms, Mrs Donovan?' she asked as she helped the woman lift Casey's buggy through the doorway.

'Oh, sorry, I forgot!' Mrs Donovan trilled, grabbing Jesse for a kiss before she shot out of the door. 'I'll bring them next time!'

Emma unfastened the cover of Casey's buggy.

When Mrs Donovan had collected her children the day before, Emma had made a point of asking her to put in nappies, formula and spare clothes as the other parents did.

Yet again the only thing inside Casey's buggy was the smiling baby.

Teething Problems

Emma was rushed off her feet the whole of that first week. Every minute was packed with deliveries of food and supplies, learning the names and faces of children and their parents, wrestling with the computer system or working in the nursery.

It was Friday afternoon before she managed to get a minute to herself. While Pam and Maisey settled the children for their after-lunch nap, Emma took the opportunity to keep the hermit of Hawthorn Ridge on-side.

Jake looked genuinely pleased when he opened the door to her.

'Hello! What brings you here?'

If Jake was pleased, then Tiger was delighted. He patted at Emma's leg with his paw until she bent down and scratched him behind his ear.

'You're sounding cheerful, Jake! Does it mean you've had no problems so far?'

His smile faded.

'Problems? With what?'

Emma studied his expression. It didn't look as though he was joking. What was more, time spent looking at Jake Allen was never wasted.

'I wanted to make sure you haven't had any problems with the nursery so far. That little local difficulty of yours that's been up and running for a week now.

'You know, the home of all things small and noisy between eight and five daily?'

'Oh, that.' He raised one shoulder slightly. 'Nah, I haven't heard a thing.

'Mind you, Maisey gave me a pair of industrial-strength, noise-cancelling headphones to thank me for asking you about a job for her. They might have helped.'

He gave a mischievous smile.

'What about you? Have you had any teething troubles at the nursery?'

'I see what you did there.' She smiled back. 'Luckily, it's been trouble-free, though I hope I'm not tempting fate.

'The only real problem we've had

is one parent who can't remember to return her children's admission forms?'

Jake expression lost its mischief.

'I've seen that poor pale shadow, Manda Donovan, dropping children off with you. If it's anything to do with them take care. Gus Donovan is a boor and a bully.'

'In that case, Jesse and his sister are welcome at the Wishing Tree Nursery,' Emma said firmly, 'no matter how long it takes their mother to return those forms.'

'Uh-oh, stop right there. If you want to run a successful business you must never let your heart rule your head.'

'I won't,' she replied obediently.

He gave her a long, knowing look.

'Take my advice. Don't ever play poker for money, Emma.'

She frowned at him, puzzled.

'What do you mean?'

'You've no intention of chasing Mrs Donovan for those forms, have you?' He chuckled. 'Your face can't keep secrets.'

'Have you thought that it's not my

face but your mind that's the problem? You might be too suspicious.'

'There are no secrets in a village.'

Emma wanted to fly to Mrs Donovan's defence, but Jake wore a look that warned her to be careful.

'Is there anything else I should know about Mr Donovan?' she asked. 'This could be your big chance to change from Mr J.P. Allen, Hermit of Hawthorn Ridge, into Jake, the perfect next-door neighbour.'

'I haven't had anything to do with Gus for ages, but we used to employ him up at the farm.

'I wouldn't normally tell you this, but if you're going to be coming into contact with him and his family there's something you should know.

'We had to let him go.'

Emma leaned forward, her eyes wide with curiosity.

'Why?'

Jake twitched his mouth.

'As it doesn't have anything directly to do with his children coming to your nursery, I'll pass for the moment. It's not relevant.'

'It wasn't anything to do with money, was it?'

'What makes you ask?'

'It's giving me kittens, looking after the Donovan children for nine hours every day without any contact number. I can't get their mum to fill in her bank details, either.'

'So you've been looking after her children for free?' he asked slowly.

Emma swallowed, but she had to nod.

'Actually it's worse than that. I keep asking her to send some baby milk, nappies and changes of clothes, but she never does.'

Emma shook her head.

'Saying that makes me feel so mean! We're always fully stocked with everything. We can keep them both clean and feed the baby, whatever happens.

'It's annoying, though. All the other parents manage to supply an emergency bag for their children.'

'You're not being mean, Emma. You're

running a business, not a charity.' Jake spoke firmly. 'You must set firm boundaries.

'If the other parents find out you're letting Mrs Donovan get away with murder they'll all start trying it on.'

Emma was horrified.

'They wouldn't. They're all really nice.'

'Can I quote you on that? I'll bet Mrs Donovan is 'really nice', too.'

'Yes, she is,' Emma muttered

'Of course she is, because she's getting one over on you. Give her a final warning today, an extra set of forms and an ultimatum.

'If she doesn't bring them back first thing on Monday morning, complete with her bank details,' Jake stressed, 'she can take the children away with her. No more free childcare.'

Emma was horrified.

'I can't do that! The poor woman will lose her job!'

'You'll have to, I'm afraid.' Jake was adamant. 'Look, do you want me to come over and have a word with her this afternoon?'

'No! Please don't bother, I'll be fine. I've got to deal with things like this myself,' Emma said, pink with embarrassment. 'It's supposed to be my new career.

'I can hardly ask for help when the Wishing Tree has only been up and running for a week!'

'All right,' Jake replied, although his tone suggested he thought the situation was very far from all right. 'But if Mrs Donovan gives you any trouble don't try to deal with it yourself. I'm just next door, remember.'

'I will. Thanks, Jake.'

He ran his hand along his jaw as though considering something.

'As you're here, would you like to come in for a coffee? Dutch courage before you confront her?'

Emma groaned inwardly. She would like nothing better than to spend time with Jake, but this was exactly the wrong moment for him to ask.

‘I’d love to.’

She wondered if he realised exactly how much she meant those words.

‘I must get back to the nursery, though. If nothing else, I have to print out some more application forms before Mrs Donovan arrives to pick up Jesse and Casey!’

The Donovans

The weekend was spent by Emma wondering if Mrs Donovan would return the forms on Monday morning.

She could cope without emergency bags for the children, but the admission forms were vital.

It would be such a shame if she had to turn the Donovan children away. Jesse had really come out of his shell.

He had spent his first day as Madeleine's shadow. Then he'd realised that racing cars and building towers with the other children was a lot more fun than being a slave.

Madeleine was left to care for her favourite dolls and soft toys on her own.

'Not so much a lone parent, more a military dictator,' Pam murmured to Emma as they watched the little girl bark orders at her silent family.

Casey Donovan was no trouble at all. As long as she got her feeds on time, she slept peacefully for much of the day.

When she was awake she was happy to lie in her cot watching the mobiles or babbling along at nursery-rhyme time.

'It would be a shame to lose those two,' Maisey agreed as Jesse bounded in on Monday morning.

As usual the Donovans were the first to arrive. Jesse usually ran straight into the playroom to grab his choice of toy before the others arrived.

Today was different. Instead of darting past Emma, he stopped and grinned up at her.

He was waving a small boomerang.

'We've been to a party! Look what I got!' he cried, accidentally slicing it across Emma's shins in a chopping motion.

'Ow, careful, Jesse!' Emma cried. 'I'll take care of that. You can help me write your name on it so it doesn't get lost.'

She expected a struggle, but at that moment the twins arrived.

When they saw Jesse was busy they raced past him toward the playroom.

'I'm going to get the scooter!' Darryl yelled.

'No, I am!' his brother shrieked.

The scooter was currently Jesse's favourite toy. Forgetting his boomerang, he raced after them.

Emma heaved a sigh of relief and rubbed her bruise. She did not want Jesse throwing that boomerang about!

'I think you'd better take this away with you,' she said, handing it to Jesse's mother.

'His cousins are here from Australia.' Mrs Donovan was all smiles. 'They are staying with my husband's family in Stroud so we went over to see them.

'Oh, and the food! Picnics every day, takeaways every night. We haven't eaten so much in years!'

Emma could believe it. Jesse and his mother both had more colour in their cheeks.

Casey was clutching a new cuddly koala.

Seeing the Donovan family so happy was such a novelty that Mrs Donovan had been gone for a while before Emma realised she still hadn't handed over their forms, nor paid a penny toward their care.

As Jake had said, Emma's only alternative was to turn the Donovan children away. If she did that, though, their mother would lose her job.

She would give it another week.

The idea of having to harden her heart loomed over Emma like a thundercloud.

Friday morning came and so did the Donovans.

Their mother trotted off to work leaving Emma feeling like a failure. She should have demanded the forms but had not. Now she'd have to wait till evening.

Pay Day

Emma wound herself up to confront Mrs Donovan that afternoon.

The Wishing Tree Nursery was now owed a lot of money in childcare fees for Jesse and Casey.

That wasn't the worst of it. Emma was worried about the safety situation.

If there was an emergency she would need contact details.

It was time for a showdown, but her nerves were tied in such knots she could barely touch her lunch.

When Mrs Donovan was due to arrive, Emma waited in reception. She had a plan.

Jesse and Casey were usually ready to go by the time their mother arrived. Today Pam and Maisey were keeping them out of sight until their mother had signed all the forms, including a direct debit form.

Emma was going to make the woman pay everything she owed or . . . What?

Were they to hold the children hostage?

Of course not, although Jesse and Casey might love that. Jesse always made a big fuss at home time. He would live at the Wishing Tree Nursery if he could.

The doorbell rang and Emma's heart began to pound. She cleared her throat and paced across the hall to the door.

Before opening the door, she pushed her hair behind her ears, untucked it, then pushed it back again.

The doorbell rang a second time.

Emma opened the door very slowly.

'Mrs Donovan . . .' she began sternly.

The woman held out a small bunch of flowers to her, smiling.

'For you, Miss Brinkley!'

Taken aback, Emma clutched the bouquet like a lucky charm.

'Oh, er, thanks very much.'

'It's pay day today, so I called in at the village shop first.' She bent to pick up the shopping bags at her feet. 'I got Jesse some sweeties and you some flowers.'

Emma was bamboozled. She should be talking about money and contact forms, but it was hard to think with her hands full of flowers.

She followed the woman into reception.

'Put those flowers down, Miss Brinkley, because you're going to be far more interested in what I've got in my pocket. Here you go!'

Mrs Donovan drew a brown envelope out of her coat pocket and handed it to Emma.

'Take what I owe you out of that.'

Emma saw that the envelope was stuffed with money.

Of course! Trust that louse to pay his staff in cash rather than into a bank account. This way there was no paper trail to be picked up by the tax people.

'I can't rummage about in your wage packet, Mrs Donovan. You do it.'

The woman stopped talking and her glance flickered around the reception area.

'Oh,' she said. 'Have you got change?'

'I could probably find you some.'

Emma made a mental note to expand

the float she kept in their cashbox. She had assumed all the parents would find it easier to pay direct from their bank accounts.

It hadn't occurred to her that anybody would want to pay in any other way.

'I'll put down the cash and you give me the change, then,' Mrs Donovan told her, taking out her roll of money.

She laid down notes without looking at their denomination or counting them. Instead her eyes were fixed on Emma's face.

The penny, quite literally, dropped. Jesse's mum didn't manage money. She relied on people taking cash from her and then giving back the right amount in change.

Thank goodness they were honest in the village shop, Emma thought.

'Right, Mrs Donovan. If you give me one of those fivers . . .' Emma waved her finger over the sheaf of notes spread out across the woman's hands '. . . I can give you change for that.'

Mrs Donovan looked relieved that

Emma had understood.

'As long as you're sure, Miss B. Catch me while I'm flush! I'd always rather overpay than end up owing you money, mind.' She gave Emma a quick look. 'As long as you keep a tally for me.'

'I will.'

Emma wondered how she might make life easier for Mrs Donovan, then remembered she ought to be making things easier for herself and her staff, too.

She took a deep breath.

'While you're here, can I ask you a few questions about Jesse and Casey? I really must fill in these forms.'

She went behind the counter to lock the money away in the cash box.

'I can take down contact numbers in case of an emergency and details of any allergies or intolerances. I'll be able to fill in your bank details, too. That way you won't have to worry about having the right change.'

'I don't have a bank account.'

At least she had tried. Emma smiled.

'Well, that's one thing less for you to

tell me, then.'

Emma scrolled through the computer files until she found the Donovans' folder.

'All I need is their dates of birth, any special health concerns and your mobile number. I'll type it all up on here then print out two copies — one for you and one for us.'

'I don't have a mobile, and there's never anybody at home during the day. We're both out at work.'

Mrs Donovan's tone had changed.

Emma looked up. The woman was looking down at her feet.

'How about the telephone number of Carey's Cleansing?'

'I suppose that will have to do.'

Maisey appeared. Jesse was helping her push Casey's buggy out from the baby room.

'Here's my little man. Look what I've got for you!' Mrs Donovan held up a huge bag of sweets. 'Make 'em last, mind. I don't know when you'll get another!'

'That bag wouldn't have lasted me five

minutes when I was Jesse's age!' Maisey remarked, shutting the door behind the Donovan family.

'Same here!' Emma chuckled.

Emergency!

A few days later it was Madeleine who was all smiles.

'We're going into town tomorrow,' she announced as Emma said goodbye to the little girl and her mother. 'Daddy's taking me to the museum while Mummy goes shopping.'

'Trust him!' Madeleine's mum rolled her eyes. 'No more sense than a beetle, that man. The novelty of that will soon wear off, I can tell you.

'As her daddy will find out quick enough!'

As Madeleine and her mother turned out of the gate, hand in hand, Mrs Donovan arrived.

'Casey has been fractious all afternoon,' Pam shared as she brought the buggy out of the baby room. 'That's not like her.'

Emma bent to look at the baby lying in her buggy. Casey was flushed and rubbing her eyes with her hands.

'She might be coming down with something. If she's like this tomorrow you'd better keep her at home, Mrs Donovan,' Emma advised.

'Yeah, I'll see what she's like in the morning.' Mrs Donovan nodded.

'It's a good job you got those forms filled in,' Pam murmured as the Donovan family left.

Next morning Emma was pleased to find Mrs Donovan turning in at the gate before Pam and Maisey arrived.

'You're nice and early. Casey must be better then. I'm so glad,' Emma remarked.

She helped Mrs Donovan lift the buggy into the nursery.

Little Jesse trailed up the front steps behind them, dragging his feet and whining.

'This isn't like you, Jesse! Normally he can't wait to get in with the toys,' she told his mother.

Mrs Donovan had her bag perched on the cover of the buggy and was sorting through it.

'My hubby's picked up a chill,' she told them. 'He went straight to bed after his shift this morning so we came out straightaway. He can't sleep with Casey teething.'

Emma moved to look closer at the baby but at the same moment Mrs Donovan had leaned over the buggy, blocking Emma's view.

'Have you given Casey anything for her teeth?'

'Yes. I gave her a dose of Calpol about an hour ago and I've rubbed some gel on her gums.'

'Then she should be fine with us. We've got plenty of sterilised teething rings in the fridge.

'That keeps them nice and cool for hot little gums,' she added.

Mrs Donovan checked her watch.

'I'll have to go. I dare not be late for work. Would you mind taking Jesse through to the nursery for me? Ta!'

With that the woman was out through the front door and gone before Emma could take the cover off Casey's buggy.

When Emma did turn it back she found Casey was bundled up in a snow-suit with the hood pulled in around her face so that her eyes, nose and mouth were barely showing.

Emma pushed back Casey's hood and felt the heat radiating from the baby before she touched the hot, dry little forehead.

Emma looked more closely at Jesse and saw he was flushed, too. No wonder he had been grizzling.

It looked like Jesse and Casey might have the same thing that was affecting their dad, she decided.

She pushed the buggy into the sick bay. Jesse was so listless he followed her without any argument.

After taking off the little boy's coat, Emma settled him down on a beanbag with a drink of cold water.

Then she turned her attention to Casey.

The baby's eyes were closed, her long, dark lashes curved against her cheeks. She never stirred as Emma peeled back the blankets and pushed back the hood of the snowsuit.

Casey's wispy strawberry-blonde curls were lank with sweat and plastered to her head.

'You should be at home,' Emma whispered.

She plunged her hands around the baby's body to lift her out of the buggy.

Without opening her eyes Casey gave a thin, high wail.

She began scrubbing at her face with her fists.

'Oh, my!' Emma gasped in horror.

This had turned into a real emergency.

Out of Contact

If only she had a mobile number for Mrs Donovan! Emma's only hope was to stop Casey's mum getting on the works coach.

Carey's Cleansing was more than a mile from the nursery and Mrs Donovan was on foot. There should be time.

She stripped Casey down to her vest and nappy and put her back in her buggy. Then she tried to ring Carey's Cleansing.

The number was engaged. She cut the call and tried again. This time it merely rang out.

The cuckoo clock on the wall peeped the hour. The other children would be arriving at any moment.

Emma was on her own with two sick children. Pam had rung in to say she had broken a tooth and would be coming after an emergency dental appointment.

Where was Maisey?

The doorbell rang and Emma raced

over to open it.

'Oh, Jake! What's the matter? Has something happened to Maisey?'

He grimaced.

'Not exactly. She rang me because she hasn't been able to get through on either your phone or the nursery number.'

'There's a reason for that,' Emma said breathlessly, waving her handset at him. 'I'm using both phones at once as I've got a major problem.'

Before she could explain, her call was answered.

'Hello, is that Carey's Cleansing? This is Emma Brinkley of the Wishing Tree Nursery. I need to get in touch with one of your employees — Mrs Donovan. Her shift is due to start at . . .'

'I'm sorry, this company doesn't operate a messaging service,' a crisp voice replied.

'But this is an emergency! Surely —'

The line went dead.

Emma took the phone from her ear and stared at it in desperation.

Jake's voice cut through the chaos in

her mind.

'Don't panic. Maisey will be here soon. She overslept, that's all.'

Emma could have cried.

'Of all the days to do that!' she said in despair. 'I'm here on my own!'

Jake was already shrugging off his jacket and stepping into the reception area.

'Is there anything I can —'

His question was cut off by a thin wail from Casey's buggy.

'That doesn't sound right!'

'I know, and her brother is sick, too.'

Emma's nerves were worn as thin as her patience.

'I can't get hold of their mother. That was Carey's I was speaking to just then. They won't contact her,' she said in the same, brisk, heartless tone the Carey's receptionist had used on her.

Jake was incensed.

'They can't do that! Let me ring them.'

'No. I'm handling this, Jake!' Emma snapped, then flushed. 'I'm sorry. I didn't mean to be rude but I'm in charge here.

This is my responsibility.'

'True, but you'll get the blame if anything happens to that child. Have you rung the local clinic?'

'I tried, but their switchboard doesn't open until half-past eight.'

'That's nearly another half an hour away. You can't wait that long — babies go downhill fast. I'll drive her to A&E.'

He was already dragging his jacket back on.

'No, Jake! Thank you, but I can't let you do that. It'll be breaking all sorts of rules.'

'I can't stand by and watch another child die!'

He was halfway to the buggy, but Emma caught him by the arm.

'Wait! I've got to let Mr Donovan know what's happening at least. He's at home in bed.

'Have you got his phone number from when he used to work for you?'

'No, but one of our men lives next door to the Donovans.' Jake's voice was low and tense. 'I'll dial his number for you.'

He picked up the nursery phone, dialled the number then handed the receiver to Emma.

Stabbing at the console on the reception desk, she put the phone on speaker.

It only took a couple of seconds for the call to connect, but to Emma it felt like forever.

A woman answered. As far as the neighbours knew, the Donovans did have a phone, although it might have been disconnected.

She agreed to go next door and pass on the message.

Emma heard Jake gasp. Pale and tense, he could hardly stand still as they listened for any sound from the phone.

She reflected on what he had said: 'I can't stand by and watch another child die.'

What had he meant by that?

Suddenly Jake made another move toward Casey's buggy.

'Wait!' Emma cried.

In the same instant the receiver was grabbed at the other end of the line and a man unleashed a stream of bad language so fierce that Emma jumped.

'Mr Donovan, is that you?' she began.

His roaring went on, but she persevered.

'I'm sorry to disturb you, Mr Donovan, but —'

'Let me handle this,' Jake urged, closing his fingers over the phone.

Covering the receiver with her hand, she scowled at him.

'I can do this!' she hissed before returning to her call. 'Am I speaking to Mr Donovan?'

Gus Donovan used a dozen words, most of them unrepeatable, to ask who else she thought it might be.

'My name is . . .'

She never managed to tell him. With a stream of abuse about cold callers, Gus Donovan had hung up.

No Time

'That's it. I'm off.' Jake grabbed the handle of the buggy, but Emma caught him by the arm a second time.

With her other hand, she hit redial. This time there was no delay in answering. The baby's father started to shout, but Emma shouted louder.

'Your baby is sick, Mr Donovan! Very sick!'

That silenced him.

Emma's announcement had even frightened her, so she wasn't surprised at its effect on him.

It stopped Jake in his tracks, too. His hands clenched on the buggy's handle. 'Who is this?' Mr Donovan growled.

'Wishing Tree Nursery at Hawthorn Ridge. Casey wasn't well when your wife dropped her off and I think she's getting worse.

'I haven't been able to get in touch with your wife and I need your permission to take Casey to hospital.'

'Where's my missus gone?'

'She's working offsite. Her employer won't contact her for me.'

'Employer? What d'you mean?'

Horrified, Emma and Jake locked gazes.

'I — I don't have time to discuss that now, Mr Donovan,' Emma flustered. 'All I need is your permission to get Casey to the emergency department right away.'

'Stay where you are.'

The tone of his voice made Emma's blood run cold.

'Wishing Tree Nursery, you said? That place past the bottom of the high street?'

'Yes, but it would be quicker if I took her there directly.'

'No! Don't move an inch. I'm coming.'

There was a bang and Emma was left listening to a silent phone.

'Jake, what have I done?'

'The right thing. Come on, help me get this contraption apart. I'll strap the carrier bit into the car for you.'

He started fiddling with the buggy fixings.

Something was still troubling Emma.

'How could Mr Donovan not know his wife had a job?'

Jake glanced at her, exasperated.

'We've an emergency and you're worrying about that?'

Stinging under the rebuke, Emma lifted the wailing baby from her buggy.

'I'll take Casey out. That'll be safer.'

In minutes Jake had the baby seat on the floor and its chassis parked in a corner.

Shaking out the baby's blanket, he spread it in the base of the carrier like a man who knew what he was doing.

'This way you can fold it over her to stop any draughts,' he said gruffly.

He dropped his chin.

'I'm sorry I snapped at you.'

'Thank you,' Emma replied. 'People deal with stress in different ways. You were right — it wasn't the time for small talk.'

'In case you're still wondering about

Gus, if he worked a night shift and slept during the day it could work.

'As long as Mrs Donovan was careful to get back home before he woke up, he need never know.'

Jake moved out of the way to let Emma put Casey into her carrier.

'When she's strapped in you can go.'

'We can't, not yet. We've got to wait for her dad. He said he was on his way.'

'There's no time for that,' Jake said tersely. 'Come on.'

'I can't, Jake! More children are due here any minute. There won't be any qualified staff here to take care of the children if I go.

'Besides, it looks as though Jesse is suffering from the same thing as his sister. I'll have to wait for Mr Donovan so he can take both his children to the hospital.'

'I'll be here,' Jake pointed out.

'You aren't qualified.'

'Let me worry about that. Maisey will arrive soon, anyway.'

He put the carrier at Emma's feet and

pulled out his phone. Within seconds he was rapping out a command to his sister.

'Get down to the nursery. No arguments. This is an emergency. Quick!'

He turned to Emma.

'I'll wait here and explain to parents as they arrive that there's been an emergency. They can either wait with their children until Maisey gets here or take them back home.'

'Oh, Jake, bless you! That's such a help.'

'Well, don't stand there wasting time. Get Casey dressed, ready to go.'

Emma's hands were shaking as she fumbled all the poppers. All the time Casey wailed with the high, unnatural sound of a feverish baby.

Emma tried to remember the comforting words of the most recent childcare course she had been on, two years before. *These days all children are kept up to date with their vaccination programme. Nine times out of ten no childhood illness is as serious as it looks.*

What if this was the tenth time?

A Furious Father

Jake had the baby's little fur-lined snow-suit in his hand, but as Emma reached for it he twitched it away.

'What are you doing? It's freezing out there! She's got to have her coat on!'

'There's no time. Fasten her in, fold the blanket over her then drape this over the top. She'll be exposed to the fresh air for no more than ten seconds between here and your car.

'Go straight out there now, turn on the engine and get the heater going. I'll give you a minute then bring her out for you.'

'I must pick up an emergency supply of nappies . . .'

'Go!' Jake thundered furiously. 'You are taking a sick child to hospital. They will have everything there already, believe me.'

The look in his eyes warned Emma not to quibble. She ran to her car, turned on the engine and got the heater going full blast.

Then she opened the rear passenger door and made sure there was enough room to place the baby carrier inside. After that she got back into the driving seat and pressed the car's horn.

Jake covered the distance between the front door and her car in half a dozen strides.

'Do you know the way to the hospital?' he asked as he leaned over the rear passenger seat to fiddle with clips and clasps.

'Yes, I memorised the route before the nursery opened on its first day.'

Jake swore under his breath.

'This carrier's useless. One of the clips is missing and another one is cracked. Do you have any rope?'

'We've miles of play string in the playroom but no rope.'

She groaned, then brightened.

'Wait! There's some in the old outbuilding. But you can't use anything from there — you said it's full of rats!'

'Emma, this is a matter of life and

death!' Jake yelled, storming off.

It couldn't be, Emma thought. Please . . .

'Poor little thing.'

Emma twisted around in her seat to try to comfort the crying baby. Casey wouldn't be comforted. She kept wailing.

This was unbearable but, then, it would be worse if Casey went quiet.

Jake arrived back at the car with a hank of dirty, evil-smelling rope in his hands.

'I'll lash it to the seat as best I can, but you must drive carefully.'

As he bent down to work on the carrier, a vehicle tore down the road toward them. It screeched to a halt on the double yellow lines opposite the nursery.

A huge man erupted from the driver's door. Striding across the road, he roared out a challenge.

'Oi! Is that my Casey?'

Jake, absorbed in securing the baby carrier, showed no sign of seeing or hearing the new arrival.

Emma got out of the driving seat,

sagging with relief.

'Thank goodness you got here . . .' she began, but Gus Donovan wasn't listening.

Rounding the back of Emma's car, he caught hold of Jake around the waist. He yanked him backwards and pulled him out of the car.

Jake had no chance to defend himself before Mr Donovan swung a punch at him. It connected with a sickening crunch.

Frozen with horror, Emma watched as Jake staggered back, his hands over his face.

If the rear passenger door hadn't swung shut by itself, the furious father would have had room to reach inside the car.

Its slam shattered Emma's trance. She leaped back into the driver's seat, threw the car into gear and roared away.

Car Chase

Three things struck her instantly. Jake had told her to drive slowly; Mr Donovan's SUV would soon catch her in her little car; and should Casey's carrier be rattling like that?

This last worry was greatest. Reaching the village shop, Emma turned into its car park.

What was the worst Mr Donovan could do if he caught up with her?

The picture of him hitting Jake was indelibly printed on her mind.

'If he snatches Casey and takes her to hospital, that would be a good thing,' she told herself.

She jumped out of the car, leaving the engine running, to check Jake's handiwork. The baby carrier seemed stable.

Emma ducked out from inside the car's interior, expecting to see the SUV blocking her exit from the car park.

It wasn't there.

Without waiting to wonder why she

couldn't hear Gus Donovan shouting, she jumped back into her car and drove slowly to the exit of the car park.

Before pulling out, she checked in both directions. Activity on the high street seemed perfectly normal for this time on a weekday morning.

There was no sign of Mr Donovan, his SUV or Jake.

All Emma could see was the odd car tootling along, Tiger's nose poking out from the gate of Plum Tree Cottage — and Maisey, using a mop and bucket on the pavement outside the Wishing Tree Nursery.

That could mean only one thing. Blood!

Emma threw open her car door again and began to get out, but Maisey had caught sight of her.

'For goodness' sake, Emma, get going! Gus shot straight past while you were wasting time there in the shop!' the girl yelled.

Stinging at the imputation that she would have stopped for anything other than an emergency, Emma got back into her car.

She drove as carefully as she dared to the local hospital.

The little baby's obvious distress made her long to put her foot to the floor. She had to fight the impulse with everything she possessed.

As she rounded the last bend, her heart sank. There was a police car parked across the road and it was completely blocking her way.

Emma rolled down her window as the policeman began to talk.

'You'll have to turn back —'

'I have to get this baby to hospital! Now!'

His face changed as he heard Casey's cries.

'OK, but there's been an incident, miss.'

The policeman began speaking into his radio.

'I've called an escort for you,' he told her a few seconds later.

Even before he finished speaking, a

police motorcyclist had roared into view. Emma was instructed to pull in behind the bike and follow it into the small hospital's car park.

The hospital parking area was packed with cars, but many of them seemed to have passengers. No doubt they were unable to leave because of the roadblocks.

Emma was directed toward a fire door at the rear of the main building.

Her hands were shaking so much she couldn't untie the knots Jake had used to secure the baby carrier. The police motorcyclist had to help her.

After Emma had been fumbling over the job for what felt like hours, he managed it with ease.

'What's the cause of this incident? It's not Mr Donovan, is it?'

The policeman looked at her warily.

'Why do you ask?'

'This is his baby,' Emma announced as he lifted the carrier out of her car.

'Are you the mother?'

Emma shook her head.

'Then I'll take her,' the policeman told her. 'You get straight back inside your car, lock the doors and stay there.

'Don't move until I get back. You'll be needed to help us with our enquiries.'

Emma did as she had been told. She watched the policeman hammer on the fire door.

It was opened straightaway by a nurse and the policeman carried Casey and carrier inside.

It was only now Emma had time to notice that she was in big trouble.

She had parked haphazardly, it seemed, with her car's nose up against a bank of large signs.

Park in marked bays only.

Find a space before purchasing a ticket.

CCTV in operation.

Fire Exit: Keep Clear.

Oh dear, she thought. She had broken every one of those rules, and right under a camera, too.

A Casualty

'We'll let you get away with those parking violations just this once,' the friendly officer said when she took Emma's statement later.

That didn't stop her feeling awful as she drove home. All the hospital would tell her was that the baby was 'stable' and that she was getting the best possible care.

Emma kept having awful flashbacks to Gus Donovan hitting Jake — and the sight of Maisey mopping up afterwards.

She was so worried about Jake and Casey that only one thing managed to worm its way into her consciousness — the horrible smell that was filling her car.

The second she pulled up outside the nursery she leaped out into the fresh air.

Pulling the coil of rope from the back seat, she carried it to the old outbuilding, opened the door and threw the rope inside as hard as she could.

'You'll need to scrub your hands well,' a familiar but muffled voice said as Emma backed away from the outbuilding. 'How's the baby?'

'Jake?' Emma turned round.

Then she stared at him, wide eyed.

'Your face!' she gasped.

'Doesn't look that bad, does it?'

Emma recovered quickly enough to lie.

'No, and it'll heal. It can't have been easy for Mr Donovan, finding out his wife had a job and his children were sick.

'All the same, he shouldn't have done it. Let's go inside and I'll see what I can do.'

'No need. I let your friend, Pam, practise her first-aid on me. She's stuffed at least half a mile of cotton-wool up my nose.'

'Oh, dear.' Only the sight of Jake's poor, battered face stopped Emma smiling. 'Did it stop the bleeding?'

'No idea, but it gave her something to do while we were watching Jesse.'

Emma had forgotten the poor little chap.

'How is he?'

'No worse. Maisey and Pam are taking care of him.

'One sits with him while the other amuses the children in the playroom.'

Emma smiled.

'It sounds like the system works. How about you?'

'I've been keeping out of sight. Don't want to scare the little ones.'

'Good idea. It must have been a lucky punch,' she added as his face fell. 'Want a cup of tea and something to eat?'

'Tea, please, but no food. Gus Donovan managed to loosen a couple of teeth as well!' He gave a lopsided smile.

The day disappeared in looking after the children, getting Jesse a video consultation with the clinic and checking on Jake.

In the afternoon Emma left Pam and Maisey in charge of the children still at the nursery. She defrosted home-made tomato soup and took it to Plum

Tree Cottage.

'I'm going to wait for Mrs Donovan outside Carey's Cleansing so that I can drive her straight to the hospital to see Casey,' she told Jake. 'She needs to know Gus has found out about her job before she gets home, too.'

'I'll come with you.'

Relief flooded over her.

'Would you mind? I think you should get looked over by a doctor. They might be able to prescribe some strong pain-killers.'

It was Jake's turn to look relieved.

'That would be good. You don't mind?'

'It's the least I can do after you've been such a support.'

Driving might be all she could do in the future if the nursery closed because all the children were off sick, Emma thought grimly.

Escape!

Emma and Jake decided that, as there would be a wait at A&E, she would drive him there first.

They took Jesse there, too, so that he would be in the right place when his mother arrived to see Casey.

Emma also felt happier to have him in the casualty department. If he started feeling worse then help was at hand.

After both Jesse and Jake were booked in, Emma drove on to Carey's Cleansing to wait for Mrs Donovan.

Once she had parked, Emma took out her phone to search for the nearest women's refuge. Mr and Mrs Donovan were unlikely to be playing happy families after what had gone on today.

'And I'm the reason Gus found out about her job,' she berated herself.

When Mrs Donovan stepped down from one of the company minibuses, Emma got out of her car.

She decided it was best to come

straight out with the bad news. Better to do it quickly and face Mrs Donovan's anger than to inch around the problem.

'Casey's been taken to hospital, I'm afraid, Mrs Donovan.'

Manda Donovan went white.

'It's not a chill. It's measles, but they're taking good care of her,' Emma went on. 'Unfortunately we were so desperate to get in contact with you that your husband found out about this.'

She gestured toward the offices.

'Oh, no!' Mrs Donovan cried. 'Not already! I was trying to save up. What am I going to do?'

'Right now the most important thing is to get you to Casey.' Emma opened the car door. 'Jesse is at the hospital, too. He almost certainly has measles, but so far he's only hot, tired and grumpy.'

'It was going to Stroud that did it,' Mrs Donovan mourned. 'I knew we shouldn't have dragged the kids all that way.

'Gus should have gone to visit them on his own. Where is he now?'

'The police took him away,' Emma told her as she drove out of the office car park.

'For how long? Will I have time to grab a few things from home before he gets back?

'When Gus started working nights it was my chance to get some money together and escape.' Her voice shook. 'Things were going well, but now I'll lose a whole week's money. All that work for nothing.'

'Don't worry. You'll be paid for the time you've already worked,' Emma reasoned.

'Not after deductions. I lose money every week for different reasons. Deductions for supplies or equipment . . .'

'You have to pay for those?'

'Of course. Everybody does if they want to work for Carey's Cleansing.' Mrs Donovan spoke as though she was explaining to a child. 'This week's money will be used up for sure.'

'We'll see about that,' Emma said firmly.

She was so angry at the thought of Mrs Donovan losing money that she couldn't wait to confront the horrible man again.

This time she would be sure to take along her secret weapon. Jake.

'My mum and dad have been telling me to leave Gus since before Jesse was born,' her passenger confided. 'Things got so bad that I'd made up my mind to do it. That's why I got this job, to try to put a bit by.

'As soon as I could afford it I was going to take the kids and run.'

'Ring your parents right now,' Emma urged. 'Use my phone. It's in my bag.'

Mrs Donovan's face lit up. She grabbed the mobile and got through in seconds.

Emma concentrated on her driving and tried not to listen, but the joy on both sides was obvious from Mrs Donovan's voice.

It was hard not to smile as well when the call ended and she was given the highlights.

'They say me and the kids can move back home straightaway! Mum'll meet me at the hospital.

'We'll only have the clothes we stand up in, but we'll have got away. That's the main thing.'

'If your husband has actually been arrested and taken off to Gloucester I'm sure you'll have time to pick up a few things from your house.

'I could give you a hand, if you like. That would be quicker.'

'Would you?'

'Of course! And we don't need to worry because it just so happens that my next-door neighbour knows your husband,' Emma said innocently. 'If Mr Donovan should happen to turn up they can chat about old times while you and I are packing up all your belongings.'

'Are you sure that'll be OK?'

'Perfectly.'

* * *

When Emma told Jake about Mrs Donovan's decision to escape, he agreed to help.

'Violence is never the answer, though,' he told her on their drive home from hospital. 'Do I look as though I would enjoy hospital food? I've thought of a much better way of getting back at that man.'

Emma glanced at him and raised an eyebrow, waiting for an explanation.

In response Jake rattled his new bottle of pills at her.

'I can't drive while I'm on these painkillers, but there are plenty of people at Hawthorn Ridge Farm who can. They must all have had trouble with Gus Donovan over the years.

'We know where he lives, after all. If Mrs Donovan's parents don't object to me redialling their number on your phone, I plan to tell them I'm sending a vehicle round to transport all their daughter's possessions to their house.'

There was a mischievous lilt to Jake's voice.

Emma glanced across at him again.

He was grinning.

'If Mrs Donovan wished to strip Gus's house down to bare walls and floor-boards I'm sure my farm staff would be delighted to help, Emma!'

Invalid Diet

Now Emma was exhausted. She hadn't stopped all day, what with the panic of the children and ferrying Jake and Mrs Donovan between home, work and hospital.

After that she'd helped a small team from the farm move Mrs Donovan and Jesse to her parents' house.

'And I'm not finished yet,' Emma muttered as she cleaned round the nursery that evening.

In the kitchen she put milk, frozen berries, oatmeal, vegetables and her soup-maker in a cardboard box and carried it next door.

Jake threw open the front door, but dashed immediately down the hall, calling over his shoulder as he went.

'Can't stop. Bad timing! Come in.'

Something photographic, she assumed, following him into the kitchen.

He then went out into the garden.

As she slid her box of provisions on to

the kitchen table, she had the feeling she was being watched. Turning round she saw an open laptop on one of the work surfaces.

An instantly recognisable, handsome man was grinning at her from the screen.

'Well, hi! I hope you aren't Miss Brinkley. A neighbour like you would be wasted on Jake!' Hollywood heart-throb Will Heath purred, confirming everything Emma had read about him.

'I'm only delivering a few things for Jake to eat while he's recovering,' she replied.

'He won't tell me how he got in that state.' Will laughed. 'I bet he was protecting your honour.'

He gave Emma a slow, seductive smile and she began to melt. No wonder this man had a following of millions — he was gorgeous.

Then he ruined the effect by opening his mouth.

'How's your bedside manner, Nurse? I've suddenly started feeling hot and bothered. Do you fancy taking my temperature?'

She put her hands on her hips.

'No, thank you. I'm more of a dentist. Ask Jake's face!' she growled.

Will sucked in a breath.

'You did that?'

'Of course not.'

His purr returned.

'I like my women feisty. Shall I give you a call some time?'

This time Emma smiled.

'No, thanks, Mr Heath. I've already got your number.'

He sighed.

'Has Jake told you anything about me?'

'Not a word.'

'You can see why, Emma,' Jake said, breezing back into the house

She had managed to hold everything together until that point, but now tears welled up.

'You need to sit down.' Solid and dependable, Jake pulled out a kitchen chair for her.

With the other hand he popped a Post-it note over the computer's camera.

'Hey!' Will cried.

Jake switched off the computer's microphone and smiled at Emma.

'That man never gives up!'

'I noticed.' She sniffed.

Jake took a box of tissues from a cupboard and handed it to her.

'He has been my best friend since we were both little boys on our first day at secondary school. That's worth a lot.'

'You can't put a price on a friendship like that,' Emma agreed, dabbing her eyes.

She herself had lost contact with a lot of people once Leonard had walked into her life.

'I'm sorry about this,' she said. 'I'm stressed and overtired. I'll leave you to your video call, Jake.

'I brought you a few supplies so you've got plenty of soft things to eat. Porridge, fruit and instructions for the soup-maker so you can whizz up a few vegetables.'

'I won't say 'you shouldn't have'

because it all looks great.' Jake's hand went to his pocket. 'How much do I owe you?'

Emma put up her own hands.

'Nothing! You were being a good Samaritan. You didn't deserve to get hurt.'

He persisted but she wouldn't budge.

'OK, but if there's anything I can do for you all you have to do is ask.'

She unloaded her box on to the table.

'This was only because I wasn't sure you'd have any soft food in the house.'

He smiled.

'Guilty as charged. I'm a steak and celery kind of guy.'

Tucking the tissue into her sleeve, Emma backed toward the door.

'Anyway, I'll leave you to your chat. And your work,' she added as the alarm on Jake's phone chimed from his pocket.

'My bad timing . . .' he began.

But Emma had let herself out before she could hear what he was going to say.

A Tragic Story

'I can't believe I'm getting paid to do this,' Maisey commented next morning as she and Emma supervised children at the sand table.

'Well, it's hardly Norland College, but I'm glad you're enjoying yourself.'

'I'm glad you mentioned Norland. Now Jake and I are able to talk about it again, I'm thinking of reapplying.

'Oh, don't worry,' she added quickly, 'I wouldn't be moving to Bath until next September at the earliest. Until then I'll be enjoying the atmosphere here.

'Happy house, happy babies, as my nanny used to say.'

Not for the first time Emma had to pinch herself. She was employing a girl who lived on a huge farm and had been cared for by a nanny!

'When Jake objected to your plans I told him he was getting wound up over nothing,' Maisey went on.

'And now he has a spy in my camp?'

Emma pondered. 'It wasn't only the noise he was worried about, though, was it?'

Looking away, Maisey shook her head.

'He was wrecked after he lost Jenny and little Olivia.'

His family? So that was it.

'What happened?'

Maisey frowned.

'Well, to begin with, Jen Heath was exactly like her brother, Will.'

Emma blinked but said nothing.

'High maintenance and a laugh riot,' Maisey elaborated. 'She got pregnant by accident and, well, motherhood wasn't exactly her style.

'She'd dump Olivia on Jake or Mum and take off with her mates. Sometimes she'd be gone for days.'

'One day Olivia became ill while Jake was away in South America. Jen didn't think it was serious, but Jake is a worrier.

'He flew straight home, but by that time Olivia was really ill. He was taking them to hospital when the car skidded on black ice and Jen and the baby were killed.

'Jake has always blamed himself, especially as he got out of the car without a scratch.'

For a long time Emma could not think of anything to say.

'That's the saddest thing I've ever heard,' she managed.

'It's why he moved to Plum Tree Cottage. The farmhouse just held too many memories for him.'

'And then he found himself living next door to a kindergarten? That couldn't be good.'

Emma sighed, but Maisey shrugged.

'My brother can't expect everyone to tiptoe round him for ever. Living next door to the Wishing Tree Nursery could ease him back into real life.'

Did his sister mean that?

'Come on, Maisey. You can hardly blame him for wanting to escape from it.'

'Maybe not, but before you took me on here my life was going nowhere and it was all because I didn't want to upset my brother.

'I couldn't go to college, but I would have liked to start up a riding club for tinies at the farm. Worrying about Jake's feelings always stopped me doing anything about it, though.'

Emma was stunned. She had never thought rich people like Maisey and her family had a care in the world. Now she knew better.

'I'd have had to get permission from Jake as landlord, as well as the riding business already up there,' Maisey went on.

'And it was too painful to raise the subject?' Emma nodded.

'Not any more, thanks to you. The Wishing Tree has broken the ice as far as I can make out.

'If Jake can live next door to little children, and even help out with them in an emergency, I'm sure he could put up with them visiting the farm for riding lessons.

'School-age children already use the stables, but I had wanted to try offering a class for the younger ones.'

Emma studied her carefully.

'Are you sure you still want to go to Norland? Something in your voice says you'd miss working at the stables.'

Maisey's face worked with indecision.

'I love working with the children here, but I love working with horses, too. I even had a name ready for my riding business — Trotting Tots. What do you think?'

'I think it's hard work, Maisey, and not much of it is glamorous. The idea of jetting round the world as nanny for rich employers and enjoying their lifestyle is very tempting, however.

'I wish I'd thought of that before I met Leonard. It would have saved me a lot of grief!'

Maisey wrinkled her nose.

'Working as a nanny is always hard work whomever you work for. Having free time in exotic locations would have helped, though, that's true.'

She sighed.

'The trouble is I want to do it all!

Become a Norland Nanny, start my own business at the stables, work here . . .'

Emma knew that more than half of small start-up businesses closed soon after opening.

'Why couldn't you try doing it all? Not all at once, obviously, but I don't think Norland has an upper age limit.'

'True. I'm not expecting to go there for at least a year, anyway,' Maisey agreed.

'You're a good worker and I don't want to lose you, but most successful businesses start very small. Why don't you canvas parents who use the Wishing Tree to see if your Trotting Tots idea is likely to be popular?

'Put a note in their emergency bags to avoid wasting your time and theirs by distracting them when they call in here.

'You could try running Trotting Tots for a year or two, then decide whether or not you still want to go to Norland.'

Maisey's eyes shone.

'I never thought of that! Is there any chance you could mentor me, Emma, when it comes to the business side?' she asked shyly. 'You're doing such a good job of running this place.'

It was all Emma could do not to shake her head in disbelief.

'You're asking me for business advice? I'm only a little start-up myself!'

Maisey shook her head.

'I believe it's wise to pick up advantages wherever you can. Some of the health and safety qualifications I needed for this job are bound to be useful in the future, for example.

'My work experience here will look good on my CV, too.'

Emma was impressed.

'Wow. Ten out of ten for forward planning!'

'You don't know the half of it. I'm already sizing up advertising space.'

Maisey nodded toward the Wishing Tree Nursery's noticeboard.

'A flyer for Trotting Tots would look good on there!'

'This village could do with more small businesses. It would stop locals having to move away to find work,' Emma agreed.

Then she had a brainwave.

'One good turn deserves another. You could put a poster up at the stables advertising the Wishing Tree!'

Favourite Recipe

That evening Jake knocked on the door to return Emma's soup-maker.

'Could you let me have the recipe for that tomato soup you gave me? It was good.'

'Of course. Did you manage the roll?'

He looked embarrassed.

'I tried, but in the end Tiger had most of it. Thanks, Donovan!'

'I did think it might be a bit optimistic. I wondered about bringing you a cheese omelette, but if real men don't eat quiche then omelette must be right off your menu!' she joked.

'I do eat quiche,' he replied. 'In fact, I eat anything — when I can chew properly.'

Emma stood back and gestured for him to go into the house.

'Come through to the kitchen. I can rustle one up in a couple of minutes.

'You should buy a soup-maker. It's brilliant. It makes too much for one person so I eat some and freeze the rest.'

He pulled out a chair and sat at the table.

'The hospital said I should be back to eating normal food by Monday.'

'You don't have to stick to soup or omelette. I make a mean risotto. And a good thing to try out your teeth for the first time might be lamb kleftiko.'

Jake watched her moving about the kitchen, dropping butter into a pan, whisking eggs and grating cheese.

'Tell me more.'

'Don't you cook?' she asked.

He shook his head.

'There seems no point doing anything fancy like that when it's only for me.'

'Kleftiko is marinaded lamb, braised on a bed of vegetables. The meat falls apart.'

He looked intrigued.

'Mmm. I wouldn't mind that.'

'I haven't made it for ages because it's not a dish for one person. Shame because it's a favourite of mine.'

She stirred cheese into the seasoned

egg mixture then poured it into the butter.

She took a chance.

'Are you doing anything on Friday evening? I was going to have a friend over but she can't make it.'

He tried to smile.

'You're inviting me to dinner while I'm looking like this?'

'Why not? If you couldn't manage to eat all the kleftiko, Tiger would polish it off!'

'I'll look forward to that,' Jake replied, and his eyes told Emma he meant it.

Dinner Date

For the rest of the week Emma took a different dish around to Jake every day.

He was a quick healer, and by the time Emma opened the door to him on Friday night his bruises were fading.

The huge bouquet of pink roses and airy white gypsophila he held took her breath away.

'They're beautiful, thanks!'

'I've brought wine, too, since I decided not to drive here today,' he joked.

'Wise decision.'

He produced two bottles.

'I wasn't sure what one drinks with lamb so there's Merlot and a Soave.'

'I usually stick to white wine whatever I'm eating. Is that bad?'

'Not at all, why should it be?'

Leading him along the passageway that separated the nursery from her living quarters, Emma opened the door into a light, primrose-painted room at the back of the old chapel.

'Lots of space in here.' He looked around appreciatively.

'I fell in love with it at once.'

She took a vase from the cupboard under the sink and filled it with water.

Unwrapping the Cellophane and ribbon from her bouquet, she mixed up the flower food then arranged the roses and gypsophila before placing the vase in the middle of her kitchen's scrubbed oak table.

'The only thing I wasn't keen on was the view from this window.'

Jake joined her at the sink.

'The other side of my wall isn't very inspiring, is it? You could take up the row of flagstones closest to it and put in some climbers, I suppose.

'You can get self-adhesive tags to fix netting against the stones and a couple of attractive ivy plants would cover it within a few seasons.

'It'd be a haven for wildlife. Birds would nest in there and bees love ivy flowers. The berries feed birds in the winter.'

Emma turned to look at him as he spoke, her smile growing wider.

'I had been thinking the same, but I was going to plant clematis and grape vines. Not for the fruit, but because little children find berries as irresistible as birds do, so I couldn't risk any accidents with ivy.

'It's also one route round to the fire assembly point so it has to be kept clear.'

He shrugged.

'No problem, that alleyway must be at least four flagstones wide. Take out one and there would still be more than enough room for people to walk along it.

'We can measure it properly later, if you like. Did you want help planting it all up?'

She smiled.

'Now it's very funny you should say that. I had intended growing trailing plants in containers along the top of the wall.

'When I discovered my neighbour on the other side had raised an objection, however, I dropped the idea in the interests of good-neighbour relations.'

'Greenery muffles sound,' he argued, 'and I like plants. I could help you make sure it's all safe and secure.'

'That sounds perfect. I was going to put in simple things like nasturtiums so they could trail down, and clematis at the bottom, which I'd train upwards.'

'Climbers take a season or two to get going. Here's an idea, although it's a noisy one!' Jake laughed. 'Why not let your children paint a mural on the bare bits of wall? Under supervision, of course.

'You and they will be able to enjoy their artwork for a couple of years. By the time the artwork is fading the artists will have moved on to school and the plants will cover their flaky paintwork.

'If you have your climbers growing on netting it would be easy to lift the whole thing away from the wall and lay it down if you want to put on a fresh coat of whitewash.'

For the next few minutes they talked easily about Emma's plans for the Wishing Tree, Maisey's excitement at her new job and Jake's progress with his art prints.

Emma had been afraid there might be awkward lulls between Jake arriving and the food being ready, but everything was fine.

She dished up their meal, which turned out perfectly because lamb kleftiko was pretty much foolproof. This was the reason she had chosen it.

It had been the first remotely posh dish she had mastered and Leonard had claimed it had won her his heart.

Despite that it was still one of Emma's favourite recipes.

Most of the preparation had been done the night before. Once it was in the oven that was it.

'I hope you're hungry, Jake.'

'I've been starving all afternoon!'

'Phht!' she spluttered. 'Please say you're joking! I don't expect that level of dedication.'

'It was the lovely smells wafting out through your kitchen window that did it. Tiger's mouth has been watering, too!'

Emma took her seat opposite, breathing in the sweet fragrance of the bouquet.

'Thank you again for the flowers. They are lovely. I really didn't expect anything.'

'Nobody should turn up for dinner empty-handed,' he told her firmly.

'Tell me about Tiger.' Emma handed him a basket of soft rolls. 'Why is he a mongrel? I thought farm dogs were all collies.'

'My family has strong links to the Urchins Wildlife Sanctuary. Maisey happened to be working there part-time when Tiger was handed in as an abandoned pup.'

'You and he make a great team,' Emma remarked.

'It wasn't always like that. I was in a dark place when Tiger turned up. It had only been six months since I lost my wife and daughter. Someone might have told you.'

She nodded slightly, bracing herself for what he might disclose.

To her relief Jake kept talking.

'At that time there didn't seem to be

any point to anything. Then Maisey fed me some story about being too busy herself to carry on raising Tiger by hand, so I took on the job.

'He has stuck to me like Boltac ever since.'

'Boltac?' she queried, puzzled.

He laughed and the heavy cloud Emma had been desperate to avoid dissipated.

'It's the stickiest substance known to man. Up at the farm we put it on the trunks of trees in autumn. It catches pests creeping up to spend winter in the fruit buds.'

'I have a lot to learn about country life.'

'Why bother?' Jake shrugged affably, 'You'll never need that little nugget of information, will you?'

'Ah, that's where you're wrong, Jake Allen! I plan to plant fruit trees with the children. I've been reading all about them.'

'And you haven't reached the bit about Boltac yet?' he teased.

‘I want something that will look good all year round. Apple trees seem to fit the bill. What do you think?’ Emma asked.

‘Sounds perfect. If you get little ones they won’t grow to much more than a couple of metres.’

‘Good. I’ve room for two or three, I think. They are a nice shape, have pretty flowers in spring and there’s the fruit. We can hang more bird-feeders, too.’

‘Good thinking. If it wasn’t for the children you could try growing mistletoe on them, too.’

Emma blushed.

‘I’m serious!’ Jake went on. ‘There used to be tons of it around here because there were lots of old orchards.

‘Mistletoe loves fruit trees, but lots have been grubbed out recently. That’s why we’ve planted a new orchard up at the farm.

‘I’m going to try pushing some ripe mistletoe berries into the bark of some of them, then we’ll be doing our bit to maintain local tradition.’

‘You’re not just a pretty face, are you?’

Emma teased.

He gestured toward his bruises.

'Not right now!'

'Oh, I wouldn't say that.'

She blushed again.

'Really?' Jake was looking at her in a way nobody had ever looked at her before. Not even Leonard.

Especially not Leonard.

She was very glad she was sitting down. The blue of Jake's gaze was making her feel weak at the knees.

'Emma,' he said softly, putting down his fork.

And that was when the doorbell rang.

Three's a Crowd

Emma could have screamed. Jake had drawn back from her like the sea from the shore.

'Were you expecting anyone?'

'No. Whoever it is I'll get rid of them,' she muttered, trying not to grit her teeth as she jumped up from the table.

Dashing down the hall, she flung open the front door, ready with a terse 'not today, thank you!'

Maisey stood outside brandishing a bottle of Prosecco.

'Surprise!'

Emma's forced smile was wide, even if it didn't reach her eyes.

'Maisey!' she said loudly enough for Jake to hear. 'Are you celebrating?'

'No, but you should be! Mum saw Mrs Donovan's dad in the shop. He was telling everybody the good news. Baby Casey is out of hospital and back home with them!'

Emma's bad humour vanished in an

instant.

'Oh, that's brilliant!'

Maisey hadn't finished.

'Manda Donovan is working with the Domestic Violence Unit to bring a case against Gus. Mum was so pleased she bought this bottle for Jake. I came down to deliver it, but he's not there.'

'Come on in! We were just having dinner.'

Maisey hesitated.

'Hi, sis,' Jake called from the kitchen.

'Oh, OK. Get out an extra glass, bro!' Maisey breezed on in, leaving Emma to follow in her wake.

'You've cooked lamb kleftiko? You lucky thing, Jake! Mum has only done us a vegetarian curry.'

'I like vegetarian curry,' Emma said appeasingly.

'Yes, but it's not very filling. I was ravenous before I came in here, and the smell of your dinner is making things ten times worse.'

She cast a gaze around the room, taking in the pear and almond tart waiting on the side and the wine bottles.

Any romantic thoughts Emma might have had vanished. There was nothing for it but to bow to the inevitable.

'Would you like some, Maisey?' she asked with another forced smile.

'Of course she would. It's my little sister's aim in life to make things awkward for me, isn't it?'

Jake was staring hard at Maisey. She returned his gaze for an age, gave one last, longing look at their dinner and started backing toward the door.

'Nah, I should go.'

'Rubbish! Sit down, Maisey. The two of us could never finish all this, and it's always nicer hot than cold.

'I can save a bit for Tiger, Jake.'

'You might as well,' he said heavily.

When Emma frowned at his tone, he shrugged.

'I mean, now Maisey has invited herself in she might as well stay. We'll have the fizz instead of the Soave to toast the news about little Casey,' he added with real pleasure.

'Mmm, lovely!' Maisey said as Emma slid a plate of lamb and vegetables in front of her. 'You're a brave woman, giving my brother his signature dish!'

Emma turned an accusing glare on Jake.

'You said you didn't cook!'

'I don't, not as such. I follow a recipe I was given years ago when I was working in Greece. I can't be spontaneous.

'This is what I call cooking.' He gestured at his plate.

It was Maisey's turn to be indignant.

'What? You always told us you made up that recipe yourself!'

'Whatever. Eat and enjoy.' Emma sat down to finish her own meal.

'Hang on a minute. In all the excitement we've forgotten to toast little Casey!'

Jake stood up and carried his empty plate to the sink. Returning to the table, he popped the Prosecco's cork and filled their glasses.

'Here's to Casey Donovan. May she live a long and happy life.'

‘Hear, hear.’ Emma and Maisey raised their glasses and clinked them with his.

Once the bubbles had been sipped, Maisey closed her eyes as the first mouthful of her dinner slipped down.

‘This is what I call real food! We haven’t had a proper Sunday dinner at Hawthorn Ridge since . . .’ she stopped, then added quickly ‘. . . for such a long time.’

Emma concentrated on finishing her meal to avoid looking at Jake.

She wondered if this new, silent tension over the dinner table was due to Maisey’s unexpected presence or because Jake’s late wife had been chief cook up at the farm.

The rest of their meal was interrupted by the trill of Maisey’s phone.

‘Hi, Mum!’ she exclaimed. ‘Yes, I found him all right.

‘He —’ she began, then registered the horrified looks Emma and Jake were giving her.

With a quick reassurance for her mother, Maisey ended the call.

'Go,' Jake said. 'Get back home to your vegetarian curry.'

'I'm too full to eat it now. And I'll miss my pudding!'

'Don't worry, I'll pack up a slice for you,' Emma told her. 'Have you got custard at home?'

Maisey stuck out her lower lip.

'Doubt it. Mum always makes that egg stuff.'

'Then take this.'

Emma grabbed a tin from the cupboard and handed it over.

'Don't leave yourself short, Emma,' Jake warned.

She guessed his concern wasn't entirely selfless. He might be fearing the prospect of not having any custard with his own pear tart.

'Don't worry, Jake, I've made ours. It's that 'egg stuff' your mum makes. Complete with vanilla seeds.'

'You'll get fat, bro!' Maisey called mockingly as she left, carrying her prize of tart and custard.

One Kiss

Once Emma returned after saying goodbye to Maisey, she dished up their pudding. They ate in silence until Jake said how much he enjoyed the pear tart.

That gave Emma the courage to ask him something.

'You know what you said about looking people up on the internet?'

'Yes.'

'I hadn't researched you until you said that. Honestly.'

He stilled, obviously wondering what she was going to say next.

'It's just that, with your history of investigative journalism and Mrs Donovan's problems with Carey's Cleansing . . .'

His expression relaxed.

'You think there's something worth investigating?'

'I don't think, I know. What sort of employer refuses to give a woman a message when her baby is sick?

'Or charges them for the supplies they

use in their work and finds millions of little ways to dock their pay?'

Jake shook his head.

'Unfortunately there are people like Colin Carey all over the world. They just say it's a tough life in business these days.'

'It's always a tough life when you're a parent like Manda Donovan!'

Jake nodded. Emma's heart went out to him. She couldn't stay silent any more.

'I did end up reading about your family. I'm sorry. I couldn't help it.'

'That's OK,' he muttered.

'It explains why you weren't delighted about this place.'

To avoid looking at him, Emma dissected her pudding into ever-smaller fragments.

'I wouldn't have tried to bring the nursery back to life if I'd known.'

He clicked his tongue.

'That's stupid! The whole village was glad when it came out that Miss South wasn't going to sell up. If she had, this place would have become another holiday let.'

He took a last sip of wine.

'Or a developer would have demolished it, and fitted in a few 'executive' homes that no local could have afforded.

'You've saved Hawthorn Ridge from that and me from multiple neighbours.'

'One neighbour must be more than enough for the hermit of Hawthorn Ridge!' she tried to joke.

Their eyes met.

'I'm beginning to think so, yes.'

'Then I'm sorry for it.'

'I didn't mean it in a bad way, Emma.' He reached out and patted her hand.

She waited, but he drew his hand away again.

'I'm sorry, I should go.'

He didn't say why and Emma couldn't ask.

When they reached the front door, he turned and smiled.

'Thanks. I've had a great time, made all the better by the news about Casey.'

Before she knew what was happening, Jake put his hands gently on her shoulders.

Drawing her toward him, he placed a chaste kiss on her forehead.

'Oh!' was all she could say, suspended in the sweet moment.

Drawn by a magnetic force, they moved together, Jake slipping his arms around her.

Emma leaned into his warm strength. As though in a dream, she lifted her face and closed her eyes.

Their lips met in a delicacy of pears, Prosecco and vanilla.

Emma was swept away until a wave of guilt washed her up on the hard gravel beach of reality.

Taking a deep breath, she moved her hands from his waist to his shoulders. Then she stepped back.

'You're right, Jake. I think you should go,' she breathed.

He nodded, but for long moments his gaze held hers. Then he turned and left.

Emma closed the door and leaned back against it heavily.

A wind was rising outside. As it prowled around the house she relived the kiss.

She wasn't sure which of them had made the first move, but that didn't matter. They had kissed. That was enough.

The memory of that sensation was still turning her insides to jelly.

'This is no good for either of us,' she scolded herself.

She had sworn never to get involved with another man as long as she lived. One broken engagement had been enough.

Jake's personal disaster made her problems seem insignificant.

And yet he had kissed her. Or had she kissed him? The thought ran through Emma like an electric shock.

What had she done?

Jake didn't seem like the sort of man to tell his awful friend, Will. But what if he told his sister?

Maisey Allen would never let her forget this.

Storm Brewing

Clearing up the kitchen was carried out on autopilot by Emma. As she went to close the kitchen curtains, she heard the bird-feeders outside dancing in the breeze.

She had been so busy getting ready for Jake's visit that she had forgotten to top them up. Now they were grating and squeaking against their metal hanging hooks.

After Jake's warning about rats, Emma took them down each evening and stored them in a rodent-proof bin.

She decided to fill the feeders up now, while she thought of it, before putting them away. Then she wouldn't need to waste time filling them in the morning.

She opened the door leading from the kitchen into the alley.

A savage wind funnelling down from Hawthorn Ridge nearly ripped it from her hands.

Looking toward the high street, along

the flagstone alley between her house and Jake's, Emma saw that party bunting strung along the eaves of the Legion Hall had broken free. Coloured triangles flew in the gale like the tail of a giant kite.

Emma filled the bird-feeders as fast as she could, all the time fighting the urge to look up and over the wall to Plum Tree Cottage.

Everything she did was measured against what Jake might think if he looked out and saw her.

This was stupid, she thought, risking a look up. To her right the black shapes of the beeches at the top of Hawthorn Ridge danced in the wind, branches flouncing as they rocked to the beat of the storm.

Closer to home the old Wishing Tree joined in the dance.

Emma squinted against the wind. Miracle of miracles, she could see the white plant label she had tied on to it.

Her wish was still attached, flipping and spinning like a minnow in a stream.

'I hope that wish goes on working

its magic,' she whispered, scanning the stormy sky.

The upper storey of Jake's house was in darkness. He wouldn't be giving her a thought.

Why should he, just because they had kissed? A man like Jake, good looking and kind, must have kissed dozens of women in his time.

She began pouring seeds from the bag into the first feeder. The lightest grains spun away into the dusk, which made her think about rats again.

Turning her back to the breeze, she made sure all the bird food went into the right place rather than bowling away.

It was a night to be indoors. When the lid was finally fastened on to the metal feed bin, Emma hurried back inside.

She toured her house from top to bottom, making sure all the windows were fastened and no doors were left to bang.

Then she retreated to the nursery office with a mug of hot chocolate, to go through her paperwork.

No child apart from Jesse and Casey

had yet come down with measles. With every day that passed it seemed more and more likely that the Donovans would be the only family affected.

That was a relief, but Emma wasn't completely reassured. Imagine if all the children had fallen ill and been kept at home!

The nursery's running costs would still carry on mounting up. Her staff needed to be paid whether they were looking after no children or a dozen.

If Maisey was going to be relying on her for business advice, Emma ought to check how well she'd be covered for loss of earnings.

She had taken out all kinds of insurance, but that didn't mean her business was safe. Insurance companies were reluctant to pay out if they could possibly help it.

Emma pulled open the deepest drawer of her desk. She pushed her fingers into the hanging file marked 'Insurance', then pulled back her hand with an exclamation of surprise. She had a papercut.

As she shook the pain away, she reflected that her finances were balanced on an edge that was equally paper thin.

Her job in the building society had helped her build up a handy nest egg during her engagement, but that pot of money had been dwindling steadily since she moved to Hawthorn Ridge.

For the next hour Emma checked everything from policies to bank statements.

The storm outside ebbed and flowed around the building like an angry sea. This place was so new to her that she wasn't used to all the little sounds that made a house a home.

The clicks and gurgles of the central-heating system and creaks as the building settled down for the night were usually comforting. Tonight, however, stranger sounds were being added to the quiet murmur.

Hard gusts rattled the window-panes. A metallic clatter sent her running to the front of the house to look out of the glazed front door. The lid of a metal ash can went bowling down the road followed by the bin itself, bouncing along the tarmac.

She felt sorry for anyone who had to go out and about in weather like this, she decided.

On the other hand, it was almost fun to have an early night and listen to the racket rolling around outside while she remained snug and warm inside.

When she had finished her scrutiny, Emma had a clearer picture of what she could tell Maisey, but she felt no happier.

She needed a minimum of six children to turn up each day in order to cover her monthly bills. If the number of toddlers and babies fell below that she would have to subsidise this business from her savings.

Her emergency fund had been dwindling steadily during her house move. As things stood she calculated that she would only be able to stay open for eight and a half days if no children came through the door.

She might receive money from her insurance policy if the business had to close completely. It looked as though she would need to hire a solicitor to make sense of the fine print. That would be a big expense.

She decided to keep her fingers crossed and keep making the small premium payments in the hope the companies would make a big payment if she needed to claim.

'If seven children or more turn up when we open tomorrow morning that will give me an excuse to look on the bright side,' she muttered.

She made herself a mug of hot chocolate, added some mini marshmallows from her stash of treats and went up to bed.

Her bedroom was at the top of the old chapel. It included an arched, stained-glass window that glowed as she switched on her bedroom light.

The gold curtains that covered the lower half of the window complemented the rich ruby, emerald and sapphire of the glass.

On moonlit nights the window sparkled against the darkness outside, but tonight her room was plunged into darkness when she switched off her bedside light.

For a moment Emma couldn't see anything. Then, as her eyes adjusted to the light, she noticed something.

Shadows cast by the Wishing Tree were dancing wildly across the walls of her bedroom. As the pale arched shape of the window became clearer, Emma spotted tiny lights dancing high on the hill.

She got out of bed and realised they must be the lights of Hawthorn Ridge Farm, Jake's old home.

She had never noticed the lights before. It was probably because the beech trees between her and the farm buildings were being pushed aside by the wind.

Emma got back into bed, but her early night did her no good at all as she lay awake, thinking about Jake.

It seemed unfair. He'd had a tough

career as a professional photographer. To leave behind the terrible scenes that had been part of his work and come home to a wife and baby sounded like a dream come true.

To have all one's happiness stolen in a split second must be unbearable.

'I must leave Jake alone to grieve,' she scolded herself. 'I'll tell him tomorrow that our kiss was an accident. That I'd love to keep him as a friend but I'm not looking for a relationship right now.'

It was what Emma told herself, but she knew it wasn't true. A few weeks before she had been convinced she would never be tempted into another relationship of any kind with a man.

Now she knew that wasn't true, either.

'See what you've done to me, Jake Allen!' she grumbled, pulling the duvet over her head to shut all thoughts of him out of her mind with sleep.

Still, as she drifted off, she was smiling.

Destruction!

The storm fastened its grip on the house and shook it. Emma woke with a jump at three a.m.

'It's always darkest before dawn,' she told herself.

The wind grabbed the trees outside and flung them about again and again.

Emma tried to settle down, but it was hopeless. Each gust of wind sounded stronger than the last.

After thrashing about for a while she gave up. The pear and almond tart was calling to her from the fridge.

She decided to go downstairs, make herself a cup of tea and cut herself a slice.

Getting up, she pulled on her dressing-gown and screwed her feet into her slippers.

With a yawn she rubbed her sleepy eyes and meandered across the room.

As she put out her hand to her bedroom door handle there was a squealing, grinding sound from somewhere behind her.

With an almighty crash the storm burst into her room and suddenly Emma was lying on the floor.

Her room was in total darkness. It was freezing cold and snowing. Snowing?

Emma reached out and touched one of the big fluffy flakes. It was a tuft of insulation from the roof.

She tried to stand up but found herself trapped inside a basketwork of twigs.

A flare of lightning lit the sky overhead where her bedroom ceiling had been until only a few moments before.

Shawls of insulation and a lacework of branches were leaning over her. The Wishing Tree had fallen on to the house!

Emma tried moving each of her limbs in turn. They were all working and so were her fingers and toes.

She had a terrible headache and her ears were ringing, but that seemed to be the worst of it.

By wriggling and inching her way under, over and between the fallen branches, she managed to find a way clear.

She stumbled out of the bedroom door, stopped on the threshold and looked back.

Her bedroom was a black hole of autumn leaves and dust, whipped into a whirlwind by the storm roaring over the remains of the roof.

Afraid of falling in the noisy darkness, Emma clutched the banister with both hands. With her head spinning she went downstairs sideways, one step at a time.

While she was still only halfway down, a bright light arced across one of the downstairs windows.

A shadow loomed and somebody knocked on the glass.

'Emma! Emma, can you hear me?' She had never been so glad to hear another person's voice in her whole life.

'Jake, thank goodness! I'll open the front door, but it'll take me a while to get there!'

'Are you all right?'

'I think so, but my house . . . my house!'

Her feet touched down on the cold tiles of the hall. She pattered across to the door, undid the safety chain and flung it open.

The wind tried to tear the door from her hands but Jake was faster and stuck one hand through the letter-box to hold it firm.

Despite her decision to tell him she only wanted to be friends, Emma felt like throwing herself into his arms.

Jake acted for her, grabbing her in a hug that lifted her off her feet.

'Oh, I'm so glad to see you!' she gasped. 'The Wishing Tree behind the house? It's come down through the roof!'

Jake pulled out his phone.

'I'll ring the fire brigade. There are power lines down.' He spoke gruffly.

He was embarrassed about that hug, Emma decided, watching Jake walk away from her to find the best signal.

The cold darkness seeping through the soles of her feet rose up her calves.

While Jake rang the electricity board and the fire brigade, she borrowed his torch and fetched her coat and boots from the cupboard under the stairs.

The inside of her wellingtons felt clammy against her bare feet and legs, but it was better than walking in thin-soled slippers.

'I'm going to get a glass of water.' She touched Jake lightly on the arm in passing.

He was still speaking into his phone.

She put her hand to her throbbing temple.

'I have a headache,' she mouthed.

He ended his call and turned his torch beam on her face, making her squint in the glare. His fingers brushed her face and she winced.

'You've a real bump there. Did you lose consciousness?'

'No, I was knocked flat, not out. I'm fine.'

Jake wasn't fooled.

'Hmm. About as fine as I was after that Gus Donovan business. You're coming home with me.'

'I can't do that!'

'Why not? You can't stay here. It's too dangerous. Without being able to see how bad the damage is we won't know if your roof is likely to collapse.'

'And there was me thinking the power lines catching fire were my biggest worry!'

'Don't worry about that. I've told the power company,' Jake replied. 'Once they've shut off the supply, though, who knows when it will come back on? They'll be busy tonight.

'I'll go upstairs and make sure everything's safe.' He pulled a head torch from his pocket and put it on. 'Then I'll grab what I can and we'll go next door. Any special requests?'

'Yes, be careful!' she called, but he was already on his way.

She stood in the darkness listening to Jake move around the upper floor.

He was gone for ages. There was a wickedly cold wind gusting down the stairs, and at last it brought Jake with it.

'Could you shine your torch on the

stairs for me, please, Emma?'

Emma did as he asked and saw his arms were full of her duvet.

'It's not good, Emma. You can't stay here until there's been a structural survey done.

'Living with that hole in the roof would be bad enough, but its whole fabric will have been weakened. It could collapse at any moment. You're coming home with me until it's been checked.'

Sleepover

'How can I thank you, Jake?' Emma said as they traipsed next door.

Jake carried her duvet. Emma, in dressing-gown and wellingtons, held slippers.

He chuckled.

'Save your thanks until you've settled in. I'm not set up for guests, but I have collected all kinds of camping equipment during my travels. Will you mind using a sleeping-bag?'

'I'll be grateful for anything. Thank you.'

'I'm not sure your duvet will be useable again,' he commented as they reached the front door of his cottage. 'It took a direct hit from a lot of plaster, roof insulation and about half a tonne of DIY firewood!'

'Why did you bother trying to rescue it?'

'I filled it with a few things to tide you over — your handbag, some clothes . . .'

'You went through my wardrobe?'

'All I did was grab a few coat-hangers, up-end the drawers of your dressing chest in the middle of the duvet, then scoop it up. Without looking, honest.'

Though embarrassed, Emma was in no position to argue. While Jake took her belongings into the sitting-room she followed the beam of her torch into his kitchen. She filled the kettle and set it to boil.

'That'll take a long time without any electricity!' Jake called out.

'Why didn't I think of that?' Emma groaned. 'It's going to be a long night without any hot drinks!'

'We can still have those.'

'How?'

'There's a wood-burner in here and a gas hob out there.

'You'll find an old-style kettle under the sink and matches to light the gas in the drawer beside the hob.

'When you live in the country you learn not to put all your eggs in one basket — or use one fuel source for all your cooking.'

'Good idea,' Emma said as she put the kettle on to boil. 'I wish the person who had the old chapel made all-electric had thought of that.'

'They must have been incomers.' Jake's tone was grim. 'When you grow up in the countryside you automatically consider things like that.

'Didn't the builders you've had in recently suggest some alternatives?'

'Now I come to think of it, they did,' Emma said as she made the tea. 'One asked if I had a log-burner on order. I thought they were making fun of me because he said they'd put in dozens over the past few years.

'Townies can't resist them, apparently.'

'Only those townies who make it through their first winter without selling up!' Jake laughed, then coughed. 'Sorry. I shouldn't have said that.'

'Do incomers often leave without staying long?' she asked as she carried their tray of drinks into the sitting-room.

She stopped on the threshold in surprise. On one side of a softly glowing wood-burner, Tiger lay curled in his bed.

In front of it Jake had set up a lightweight camp bed. He was unrolling a sleeping-bag on top.

'If this is what you call being not set up for guests then you must have very high standards,' she commented as she handed him his mug of tea.

'Thanks. To go back to your question, people who move into Hawthorn Ridge either move out again within a year or settle here for life.'

She curled up in the armchair closest to the log-burner's cheerful glow.

'Why is that? Are the locals that unfriendly?'

'No, but incomers can be,' Jake retorted, then brought himself up short. 'I'm sorry but it's true. Village life isn't for everyone.

'There has to be give and take on both sides. If strangers aren't willing to make allowances for the lack of theatres and expensive restaurants . . .'

'Not to mention the likelihood of power cuts?'

He took a long drink of tea before answering.

'That, too. They soon feel isolated. Then, the first time the river breaks its banks and floods their house, or the slow broadband speed drives them insane, they move back to the city.'

Emma could sympathise to a point.

'I'm a good long way from the river here and I've never been much of a socialiser. I want to succeed in Hawthorn Ridge, but at least you've left me no illusions.

'I'd rather have a quiet night in than go out painting the town red. That's in my favour, I suppose,' she finished.

'That's actually a shame. Our little local playhouse can only exist if people use it.'

'In that case I'll make the effort. Have you any other advice for me about fitting in?'

'You've got most of it right already, I reckon, Emma,'Jake replied. 'You're providing a service that locals need, you're employing people who live here and you've tried to talk to everyone.'

She felt the warmth of his smile through the darkness and blushed.

'I haven't! The only people I've got to know since I moved in are you and Maisey.'

'What about the staff in the village shop? Or at the fish-and-chip shop?

'Then there are your builders. Not to mention all the mums, dads and children connected with the Wishing Tree.'

'You mean 'the bombsite formerly known as the Wishing Tree', don't you?'

She sighed, holding his torch out to him.

He waved it away.

'Hang on to that for now. I wasn't sure if you were equipped for power cuts, having come from the city. I have others.'

'Thanks. I do have one somewhere, but I thought I'd be using it outside the house, not inside!'

'It's a good idea to have candles and matches handy, too, in case batteries or bulbs fail.

'Keep your candles in the fridge. Hard wax burns more slowly.'

'You're full of great advice, Jake, but I'm not sure you'll be able to do anything about my wrecked house.

'Why couldn't that tree have gone the other way? Just my luck, I suppose.'

'Don't talk like that. You've had a narrow squeak. Thank your lucky stars those cables never set your house on fire.'

He lowered his mug.

While Emma wanted him to walk toward her, she was afraid he might do exactly that.

She held her breath, but Jake strolled past her chair with unhurried steps.

With a mixture of relief and disappointment she exhaled.

Reaching the door, he paused.

'Treat this place as your own, Emma. And remember, the damage next door might not be as bad as you think. Everything always looks ten times worse at night.'

'A tree landed on my house! How

much worse can it get?'

Emma knew she would never get to sleep. The awareness of sleeping in Jake's house, the racket of the storm and worrying about her own house kept her awake for hours.

There was no way she would be able to open the nursery on Monday morning but, if she didn't, how would those parents who relied on the Wishing Tree Nursery manage without childcare?

Exhausted, she finally drifted off to sleep.

It felt only seconds later when something woke her.

She lay in silence, waiting for the next gust of wind, but the storm seemed to have died down. Then an unusual sound came from far away behind the house.

Tiger was missing from his basket, so Emma hopped out of bed and crept off to look for him.

The dog was in the kitchen, sitting at the glass door leading to the garden.

It was barely light outside. A pair of dazzling headlights was bouncing down the hill behind Plum Tree Cottage.

Reaching its boundary fence, the vehicle swung away toward the rear of her own garden and Emma realised it was a tractor pulling a trailer.

She went to the foot of the stairs.

'Jake?'

There was no reply. He must have gone out and left by the back door, which was why Tiger was waiting there.

Emma tried a light switch, but the electricity still wasn't on. She felt awkward about being alone in Jake's home, so she pulled on some clothes and went to make a cup of tea — the cure for everything.

That was when she found his note, stuck to a tin of tea bags.

I've gone to do something about your tree. The power's likely to be off until this evening so make yourself at home.

Keep the wood-burner stoked and there will be plenty of hot water.

Lumberjack

As soon as it was fully light, Emma went out to investigate.

Tiger bounded up to the fence between the top of Jake's garden and her own. He stood wagging his tail and watching three men in protective gear attacking the poor old Wishing Tree.

One stopped work, put down his chainsaw and walked over to her. It was Jake, looking as impressive as any lumberjack.

He pushed up his visor.

'It comes to something when that tree could grant your wish but couldn't survive the storm.'

'What do you mean?'

'That little label tied to the tree. It was the first thing I saw when I went upstairs last night. It was fluttering from one of the branches that had fallen in your bedroom.'

'Oh, that?' Emma was embarrassed. 'That was just some nonsense.'

'I thought so. In case it wasn't, I put it, twig and all, on the kitchen window-sill. Did you see it?'

'No. I made tea then retreated to sit by the wood-burner.'

'You'll need a new Wishing Tree. Mum says they'll root from branch ends,' he told her, 'so I'll get her to look out a good one for you before we turn it all into logs. Then you'll have a replacement.'

'Thanks.' She spoke without enthusiasm. 'That storm has created havoc. I had local radio going on my phone until I realised I'd have to charge it from the mains.'

'Don't you have a powerpack? That's something else to put on your Christmas list along with that wood-burning stove.'

'Definitely!'

'We'll store all this wood up at the farm for you. It will need to season, which gives you the chance to get the nursery up and running again.

'I don't know if mulberry wood spits when you put it on the fire. Keep the burner doors closed, just in case, but I shouldn't think it throws out much tar.

'It won't clog your chimney in minutes like pine does.'

Emma nodded, then realised Jake was not going to be fooled.

'Nope, sorry, I haven't got a clue what you're talking about,' she admitted. 'For now I'll trust your judgement.'

'That'll do.' He smiled. 'Any chance of a cup of tea for the workers?'

'Of course,' Emma said, then sighed. 'I'd got up to fetch a slice of pear tart when the tree fell. It's what stopped me getting hurt. Do you think it's safe for me to go and fetch the cake tin from in there?'

'You make the tea and I'll fetch the cake. I still have your keys after locking up last night.' He patted his jacket pocket.

* * *

'I had a firm booked already to come and mend the deer-proof fence. They were supposed to be coming next week but I suppose they'll be too busy with emergency repairs now,' Emma said later as she handed tea over the fence to Jake.

'This *is* an emergency,' he said, dividing up the tart. 'Once we've shifted the tree we'll do a temporary repair on that part.

'If the firm you've booked tries to delay don't let the people get away with it.

'Tell them it's a health and safety issue. You've got small children to corral.'

Possibly not for much longer, Emma thought, but didn't say it aloud.

'Could you do me another favour? Go into the nursery and bring out two metal boxes from under the counter in reception.

'One of them is the cash box. The other is the file containing all my insurance documents. I need to start ringing round.'

Packing Up

Emma's insurance company sent out a firm with impressive speed to inspect the building and make it safe.

Jake disappeared, taking Tiger with him. His house and studio were still deserted when Emma got the go-ahead to move back into her home on Sunday evening.

She rang him.

'I'm up at the farm,' he said. 'I thought you'd want time to collect your thoughts. Would you like some help clearing up?'

'Please! Parts of the back wall aren't safe so I've to move everything toward the front of the building.

'We're going to be so cluttered there will be hardly any room for the children.'

'Maybe the insurance company will let you use the builders who converted some of our farm buildings. They did a great job and they didn't take long.

'You'll only need to close for a few weeks. It won't be for ever.'

'It might as well be.'

She looked around at the little tables, chairs and easels, the book corner, nature table and cooking space.

'I'd already worked out how many children I'd need to keep the Wishing Tree going. The figure wasn't zero.

'My insurance company will pay to have the damage put right, and even to let me stay somewhere while the work is done. But I wasn't covered for a total loss of earnings for maybe months on end.

'This place was perfect. Children loved coming here. Now they've lost it and I face losing everything.'

'I'll be right there,' he said and hung up.

* * *

Jake set to work, which Emma appreciated as she didn't feel like talking.

She wrapped and packed small items into crates as he stacked chairs and tables.

He called out to her.

'I need to do some phoning, Emma. Shall I make coffee at the same time?'

'Yes, please. You might bring out biscuits from the staff kitchen.'

Jake was gone for so long that finally she wandered out to find him. He was by the sink listening to his phone.

Mugs of coffee stood at the kettle. Emma took a sip from one. It was almost cold.

She rinsed the cups and reboiled the kettle as he ended his call.

'While we were packing up I had an idea,' he told her, wrapping his fingers around a fresh cup of coffee. 'I didn't want to say anything until I'd rung around to see if it was feasible.

'It is, so I can tell you. Pack up everything here and move the nursery to Hawthorn Ridge Farm until this place is fixed.'

She stared at him, incredulous.

'What?'

'I'm serious. We have an awkwardly sized studio unit up there. I rented it to a ballet teacher for a while, but her classes got so popular she moved to bigger premises.'

'Thanks, Jake, but it's one thing to offer parents a nursery they can walk to, within easy reach of the school and the shop. Access to Hawthorn Ridge Farm must be a lot more difficult.

'There's no road running over the hill. Parents can't hike backwards and forwards across the field and over the ridge twice a day with winter coming.

'It's the lack of children that will shut me down, not the lack of space.'

'Let me explain, Emma. Work out how many children you need to come to the nursery each day to break even. For every day you get fewer than that I'll make up the difference.

'What do you think?'

Shuttle Service

Closing her eyes in despair, Emma shook her head.

'I can't take your money, Jake!'

'Of course you can. What else have I got to spend it on apart from boring old bills? I know where I'd rather put my money.

'It'll be short-term help, Emma, not a handout. Keep a record and then you can pay me back when you get over this sticky patch. It's temporary.

'Don't forget, all the parents with cars will be only too happy to drive straight to the farm. The access is easy from the main road, further up the valley.

'We also have plenty of room at Hawthorn Ridge for dropping off and picking up.

'As for those on foot, you might find every one of them is ready and waiting to follow you up the hill, like the Pied Piper.'

She shook her head at his nonsense.

'I can't expect them to walk all that way. We'd have to carry the babies.

'Besides, how am I going to get that place ready in time, as well as getting the message out before we're due to open for business tomorrow morning?'

'You're overthinking things,' he replied, finishing his coffee and rinsing the cup. 'Maisey is giving the unit a quick spring clean. While I finish boxing all this stuff up, you can make a start on contacting all the parents.

'I'll get the nursery things collected, like we did for Mrs Donovan. Then Maisey and I will both help you get in touch with the parents by ringing round.'

'You're volunteering your sister again!' Emma warned, although her spirits were beginning to rise.

He nodded.

'I am. Tomorrow morning I'll post somebody where the parents usually leave their cars in case we can't reach any parents.

'Hawthorn Ridge Farm has been here longer than the village so everyone will know it. A lot of your children arrive at nine, don't they?'

'Yes, after their older brothers and sisters have been dropped off at school.'

'In that case we could run a shuttle service for the first day or two. Maisey has a PSV licence for taking kids to Pony Club events.

'She can use the farm minibus and do a run at about half-past eight.'

Emma's eyes widened.

'I can put a message on the gate explaining that the nursery has been relocated, along with my phone number,' she suggested.

'That's the spirit! I'll hang around at the gate. If anybody looks like they're going to turn away without ringing you for a lift, I'll offer to run them up to the farm myself.'

'You would do that for me?'

'Of course,' he said instantly, then paused for a heartbeat. 'I'd do it for anybody.'

'I thought you didn't like going up to the farm, Jake,' she said softly.

'I had to get over that when I went to fetch the tools to pull the tree off your house. An emergency puts things into perspective.

'My help might not be needed, remember.'

'You'll always be needed. I couldn't have managed without you,' Emma said on impulse.

'Rubbish!'

For a split second Jake's hand cupped the side of her face. Then his arm fell to his side again.

'I'm convinced there's nothing you can't do, Emma Brinkley, if you put your mind to it.'

She looked at him keenly.

'Apart from convincing Mr J.P. Allen I came to Hawthorn Ridge in peace?'

After a pause he spoke.

'You did that within a few weeks of arriving.'

It was a significant moment.

'Good,' she said quietly.

'I owe you an apology, Emma.'

'I'm not going to argue with that.'

He lifted one hand.

'In my defence, when you put in that planning application you were an unknown quantity.'

'That was no reason to assume the worst, Jake.'

'You're right,' he agreed. 'Although I've had a terrible time when it comes to women and children in the past.'

Emma had no idea what to say.

'Maisey did tell me a bit of what happened.'

'Really?' He looked wary and Emma could have kicked herself for putting it so clumsily.

'Accidents happen, but when Jenny got pregnant I was over the moon. I didn't think things through.'

He looked down at his hands.

'Jen didn't take to motherhood. Our marriage failed partly because of that, but mostly because I was away so much.'

Emma stared at him.

'I should have given it all up the minute Olivia was born. It never crossed my mind to get a proper job — one where I could come home every night.

'The trouble is, I like taking photos more than anything else. It blinded me to what was necessary.'

'Don't say that, Jake. I saw your photos of Ukraine and Pakistan online. You're brilliant! The world needs to see pictures like those.'

'It didn't do my marriage, or my family any good. Or me,' Jake added in a low voice. 'I'm finished with that kind of work now, Emma.

'Why couldn't I have finished with it back then, before I lost everything?'

'You couldn't see the future,' Emma pointed out. 'Nobody can. By the time the worst happens it's too late. Like it is for the Wishing Tree Nursery.'

He looked puzzled.

'What?'

'I told my great-aunt I'd give it six months so I'll keep going until then, but I can't really see how I can survive this.'

'You've never struck me as a quitter, Emma!'

She lifted her shoulders, let them fall

and closed her eyes in desperation.

'I wasn't, before the Wishing Tree decided to drop in on me! First Casey falling sick, now this. It's too much, Jake.'

She felt him move closer until she could feel his comforting warmth.

There was a pause, then she felt his arms slide around her. She relaxed into the strength of him as he drew her gently into his embrace.

'It doesn't have to end like this, Emma.'

She felt him rest his cheek against the top of her head. His warm stability encouraged her to lean against him.

'I think it does. Aunt Elizabeth can't be expected to support me if this business isn't viable. I'm on my own.'

'No, you aren't.'

Silence.

'I'm here,' he said at last.

'Whatever must you think of me, Jake?'

'I think exactly the same as everyone else. All the mums, dads, kids . . . everybody in Hawthorn Ridge.

'We think that you're a trier who has just hit a bad patch,' he told her.

'Anyway, this packing is nearly finished. I'll take it up to the farm while you get an early night.

'Everything is bound to look a whole lot better after a good night's sleep.'

Surprise, Surprise!

'What on earth are you doing here so early in the morning, Jake?' Emma asked as she opened the door to him the following morning. 'The children will be arriving any minute!'

'I wanted to invite you outside to see something very special. Put on your coat and come with me.'

She pulled it on obediently and followed him out into the front garden of the Wishing Tree Nursery.

There were two women standing inside the gates, holding the hands of a small child.

'Oh, no! They couldn't have got the message!' Emma started to fluster.

'They got it. It's Mrs Donovan and her mum. See?'

'And Jesse!' Emma cried, starting forward as the little boy shrieked in welcome. 'I didn't think you'd be coming back, Jesse, so I didn't let your mum know what was happening today!'

She was amazed to see that Mrs Donovan and her mother didn't look either puzzled or angry.

Jesse was bouncing with excitement.

'Emma! Look what Grandad has done!'

She followed his pointing finger and noticed a ladder leaning against the wall of the nursery.

Jesse's grandfather was on top of it, checking the ties of a huge banner.

Decorated with bunting and balloons, it stretched across the entire front of the building and was painted with three words: Save Our Sprogs!

'Seemed to fit,' Manda Donovan told her seriously. 'Because you did, Miss B.'

Emma could barely manage to stammer her thanks.

'You deserve it.' Jake put his hand on her shoulder. 'If it wasn't for you, parents who wanted to work wouldn't be able to leave the house.'

'There's a limit to how much people like us can drop everything to look after our grandkids,' Mrs Donovan's mother added. 'No matter how much we love them.'

At last Emma's heart warmed with the realisation that, yes, she was doing some good in her new home of Hawthorn Ridge.

'I'm afraid the Wishing Tree Nursery has had to move up to Hawthorn Ridge Farm until everything is fixed.'

'Don't matter. My mum and dad have a car,' Manda Donovan replied. 'They can drop Jesse and Casey off at the farm for me any time. Please don't shut the nursery! Everybody here in Hawthorn Ridge needs it.'

'That's emotional blackmail,' Emma protested a few minutes later as she and Jake waved Mrs Donovan and her family off toward the farm.

'At least you'll be having some peace and quiet for a while, Jake,' she added as they walked back into the nursery.

'That doesn't seem so important to me any more.'

'I know what you mean,' Emma said as she made them both mugs of tea. 'It must have taken Mrs Donovan ages to make that banner.'

'She didn't. All the families pitched in up at the farm. Maisey supervised.'

'Ah!' Emma waggled a teaspoon at him. 'So that's how they got hold of all the other decorations!'

Without thinking, she moved closer, intending to give him a grateful peck on the cheek.

'Thanks for making this happen, Jake.'

It was the perfect moment and felt like the most natural thing in the world, but at the last moment she stopped, suddenly shy.

She couldn't bring herself to invade the personal space of this private man.

'I don't deserve . . .' She was going to say 'you', but that felt too personal.

'. . . all that.'

'If anyone deserves our support right now then you do. The storm was something you couldn't possibly have foreseen. You were insured, so it's not as though you've been either short-sighted or stupid.

'We're all behind you, Emma,' Jake finished.

She felt a sudden flush of pleasure. Imagine Jake saying this when their relationship had started out so badly!

'Another thing,' he went on. 'If you have any trouble getting bridging finance to help you over this patch, then let me help.

'If you don't have any luck with your own bank, I'm happy to act as a referee for you with my farm's bank instead.'

'As long as you aren't doing all this because you feel sorry for me,' she fretted.

'Quite the opposite.' He grinned. 'I know a good bet when I see one.'

Emma giggled.

'Please don't come over all Colin Carey, Mr J.P. Allen!'

'Never. I've got far too much respect for you.'

Something about his low, husky tone set Emma's skin tingling.

She turned her full attention to his face.

His blue eyes were so clear and intense that she spoke before he could come out with something he might regret.

'That's good, because saying he felt sorry for me was how Leonard persuaded me to get engaged.

'I'm never falling for that line again and neither should you, Jake,' she added softly. 'I want to be your friend. Nothing more.'

'You'd be happy with nothing more than friendship?'

Colour stung her cheeks, and she couldn't meet his gaze.

'I'm sure Jenny must have left an unfillable hole in your life.'

'You're right. She did.'

'I wouldn't — couldn't — ever hope to fill that.'

'I understand,' Jake told her. 'Any woman who got tangled up with me would need to be so special she was unique. Someone who could carve her own niche in what is left.'

He looked down at her tenderly and Emma swallowed hard.

'To be honest is the only way to be. I'm sorry, Jake, I'm not a stonemason. I might not be any good at carving a niche.'

'I'm convinced you can do anything, Emma Brinkley, if you put your mind to it.' He smiled.

Emma thought about how far she had come in such a short time.

'In that case, do you fancy offering this novice stonemason an apprenticeship?' she suggested.

'When can you start?' He laughed.